Verge 2024

Verge 2024

Click

Edited by
j. taylor bell, Julia Faragher,
Isabella G. Mead and Anna Pane

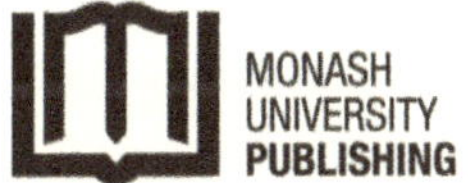

Published by Monash University Publishing

Matheson Library Annexe
40 Exhibition Walk
Monash University
Clayton, Victoria 3800, Australia
publishing.monash.edu/

Monash University Publishing: the discussion starts here

Verge 2024: Click
ISBN: 9781922979728 (paperback)
ISBN: 9781922979735 (pdf)
ISBN: 9781922979742 (epub)
ISSN: 2208-5637

Text Design by Les Thomas
Typesetting by Jo Mullins
Cover image reproduced with permission of Christopher Pane

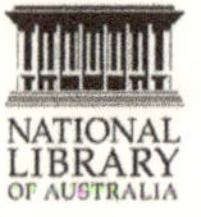

A catalogue record for this book is available from the National Library of Australia

Contents

Preface

The creative works in this collection click in entirely different ways. There are the haphazard clicks of the mouse on a web page – the hypertext, the opening of a new page or chapter. Clicks also echo in the unfastening of a harness buckle, the pinch of a clip-on earring, and the release of the safety latch on a shotgun. There is the inaudible click of thoughts interlocking together into a coherent idea and the metaphorical clicking of things into place. The onomatopoeia at the heart of the word itself forks equally towards both verb and noun, material and spiritual, objective and subjective. The click can act as both sign and signifier.

A click signifies a change, a movement from one state to another. With a click, something is altered, or settled. For Jim, in Riley Sadlier's "Going Live", the act of clicking on the YouTube video solidifies his humiliation. In Ola Kwintowski's "Freefalling", the click of the harness release after touching down on solid ground signals the end of her euphoria. A clicking sound conjures the ghost that haunts a house in Rachel McEleney's "Slab Hut Cottage", while Elena Disilvestro explores memory, dreams and reality through the tapping claws and chattering teeth of an imagined, internal creature in "Critters and Conch Shells".

Many of the poems in this collection play with sonic qualities in response to the theme: the gate closing in Stefan Dubczuk's "Exiting the Nursing Home"; the "ping!" of a phone in Pat Saunder's "lunchbreak"; a vanishing sigh in Paris Rosemont's "The Magician's Nymphalidae". Endings and new beginnings, things clicking in and out of place, are referenced in Jemma van Loenen's "Fall" and Alex Chambers' "Sleeper train, Hue to Hanoi" – a story which flirts with the skeuomorphic quality of a smartphone clicking and the symbolism thereby. Whereas other poems canvass ecological concerns and the intersection between technology and climate collapse, as in Tiffany Hastie's "I Am Named" or Timothy Loveday's deconstruction of Barthes' *Camera Lucida* in his poem "Michelet's Higher Education Shark".

The breadth of variety in the responses to this year's prompt offer new meanings and interpretations of "click". They suggest that, in all of the ways in which we are more online than ever, the term itself has evolved with those systems. Online or offline, a click can capture, it can grant access, and it can release.

j. taylor bell
Julia Faragher
Isabella G. Mead
Anna Pane

1

"thanks for doing more with less"

Dom Symes

I sign the book   "thanks for believing in me"

& my friend from school's brow collapses
like the bridge in the worst poem of all time

tho I guess it's phrases like this
which may have allowed me to cement
myself in a stable job

as one appointment oozes into the next

a year ago my buddy Jake said: *amateurism should be*
the central tenet of a healthy demos

meaning no one really knows   & even if they did
how can anyone hold such fixed ideas?

Eileen's gag at readings is to say:
they never tell you just how much of being a poet
is drinking water in front of an audience of your peers

hey have you ever heard anyone
swallow loudly on a podcast before?

not my cup of tea

   "thanks for inviting me"

I've never eaten real duck
but this fake duck is pretty fucking crispy

do you ever wonder
what's the most radical thing to ever be reposted?
& did that undercut its radicality?

like Noel says to Liam:
these lot think it's rock'n'roll
to get thrown off a ferry

…rock'n'roll is going to Amsterdam
doing your gig
  playing your music
that's rock'n' roll, right?

I can say I'm a visual learner & no one
can say I've been on Instagram too long
dissociating at terminal velocity

ASMR eye exam:
which is better 1 or 2?
how about now?
number 1?
or is it better now
with number 2?
again
number 1?
let's try number 2

  "thanks for seeing me"

if someone says "sunbeam"
I'll forever think about you Gigi
singing the bridge from "Cruel Summer"
with your airpods in lying on your sofa
while I'm writing this from your bed
on a Sunday afternoon the 22nd of October

remember Frost:

if you can keep your head
like a chicken does
when all around you are losing theirs
like a chicken does

well   now the chickens are revolting

in our meeting
my colleague called my "situation":
tertiary homelessness

which is a bit dramatic

I've got some clothes
(mostly clean) enough pants & shirts for work

"thanks for letting me crash"

I take a little bit of space
on the shelf in the fridge
between the irish butter
the kimchi & the coopers pale ales

I'm writing very minor poems now
from Tim's couch

inspired by the plastic bag from the shop
which says:

"thanks for doing more with less"

2

Going Live

Riley Sadlier

She reaches out and grabs his hand on the table, knocking the salt shaker over as she does so. He fights that initial urge to slap her hand away. This might be the last time she'll ever hold him.

"I just don't get it", he says, "how can we go from being so happy together and now you're breaking up with me? It's so out of the blue, Amanda."

He knows that he's about to cry and that his voice is starting to crack. He doesn't understand how she can go from showing him her videos on her laptop, to dumping him before she has even bothered to put it back in her bag.

"It's not as though I don't care about you", she says.

"Then don't break up with me."

She glares at him, "as I was saying. It's not as though I don't care about you, I do still love you. But school is coming to a close and my YouTube channel is really starting to take off, I have to get my priorities sorted."

"I can support you…"

"But I don't need support from you, I'm strong enough to do it on my own. I need you to respect that."

"I just, I don't want you to leave me. You've got a future lined up and I've got nothing after high school. You make me happy."

His phone is vibrating in his pocket, Amanda's eyes scan down towards the noise as she tries to ignore it. Jim hasn't realised that it's going off. His voice is getting louder and the other residents in the café are getting quieter so that they can listen in. He's begging her to stay but she cuts him off again.

"I'm so sorry Jimmy. I'm starting my journey and I want to do this alone."

He stays quiet and she grips his hand tighter.

"I'll always love you Jimmy, you're my first love and I'll never forget that."

On hearing that, Jim starts sobbing at the table. He was trying so hard to keep everything contained but that last sentence broke him. His phone continues to vibrate, now with phone calls as well as texts.

He wipes his eyes but there's no use now, once he starts crying around her, he won't stop until she's gone. He pulls his phone out of his pocket to see another phone call, he shows her his screen as an excuse to leave, "Sorry."

Getting up from his seat, he grabs his bag and runs out of the café. Finding a park bench a few hundred metres away, he sits and catches his breath. He pulls out his phone to see what was so urgent.

An all-caps text catches his eye first, "SHE'S LIVE STREAMING YOU, YOU IDIOT, STOP TALKING", and then another, "OH GOD WHATEVER YOU DO DON'T CRY", which was quickly followed by "THIS IS LIKE A HORROR MOVIE, JUST GET OUT OF THERE BEFORE YOU MAKE SHIT WORSE".

He doesn't text back or answer any of the calls. For the next twenty minutes he doesn't do anything. He resists the urge to even go on his socials because he knows that the video will be on all of them by now. A new one being uploaded as soon as the other gets taken down. On second thought, he's not even sure his friends would go to the lengths of reporting it for it to be taken down in the first place. How could he have been so stupid not to see she was filming? Her laptop camera was facing right at them.

That night he finally looks it up. Walking into the house, his Mum doesn't ask what's wrong, she just hugs him and says that it's going to be alright. She's already seen it, and once something reaches a parent's social media you know it's done the rounds.

He finds the original Instagram Live, with a caption from her saying "This is the hardest thing I've ever had to do…" because she's so brave.

The content isn't that bad. Seeing himself cry on camera, while embarrassing, could be interpreted as sweet. He may even get more attention from the girls because of it, look at how in touch with his emotions he is. It's the comments that are cruel.

By that evening she has uploaded an edited video to YouTube, adding an additional ten minutes of her commentary and explaining why she dumped him the way that she did. "I just think that, with how disconnected we all are nowadays with social media, if I could capture raw human emotion then I might be able to make a difference." A difference to what, he has no idea.

Looking through her YouTube channel it's makeup tutorials, cooking demonstrations and then his ugly crying face in a thumbnail. Anyone clicking on that knows what they are going to see.

"You're making me cry as well Amanda, thank you for this", "You're so real and authentic Amanda, it's unbelievable" and "I can't believe that you would share this with us, thank you so much!" Not all are friendly. A large number of them call her out. "You are a monster", "Trashy bitch", "Leave the little beta alone". He fights his instinct to defend her.

He thinks about putting a stop to it, at least trying to send her a message and asking her to take it down. But he sees what it's doing to her follower count, she only has twelve-thousand followers and yet this video has more than a hundred-thousand views. It might follow him around for a long time, but the traction that it's getting might convince Amanda to take him back. People are invested now, a video two months later where she graciously takes him back could really push up her followers. The longer it stays online, the more likely they are to get back together. This makes sense to him, even while the rest of his brain is foggy and unfocused.

He puts his phone on airplane mode to silence all of the sad messages and friends trying to call him. He goes to bed early that night without dinner. With the video hanging over his head he still manages to sleep well. The attention will die down soon, he just needs to get through that initial week at school.

Once the fire has calmed down he can approach Amanda and pitch her his video idea.

3

Another TED Talk, If You Like

Ouyang Yu

I talk about self-translation as a shameful act, like masturbation. I talk about writing poetry like a permanent production of failure. I talk about literature as a littering of one's literal lateral bleedings. I talk about writing as a way of living death. I talk about music that survives the ears. I talk about bilinguality as love living with love, and tongue tied with tongue. I talk about praising as a way of lifting the world and liberating the self. I talk about criticism as self-criticism and self-censorship that transform mere editing. I talk about ditching capitalism by going at the rate of one word per day. I talk about writing for the sake of writing, never submitting anything for publication, not even posthumously.

I'll talk about all that when I have time

4

On the Phone with My Sister

Dior Angel Sutherland

mid sentence you stop
there are eagles in the sky
two of them, you say, one flying so low
it could kiss the grass. there are three, usually, there most evenings
it must be the youngest, it looks like it's playing
it must be playing. wedgetails.
I see them too. outside your door the valley lifts to
a haze of burnt mountains.
they rise, dip, drive needle points to the sun
until they are swallowed. until they are completely free.

5

Slab Hut Cottage

Rachel McEleney

I fell in love with it the first time I saw it. Felt like I was coming home when I stepped on to the rickety deck. It was an old limestone block house with a bullnose veranda that stuck out like a protruding lip. Neighbours laughed when they heard it had been sold. There's a resident ghost, but I've never seen her. I've just heard the whispers in town, local gossip. A silhouette in the moonlight wandering near the house, her white dress flittering in the breeze. Or so the neighbours say. No one tells me who she is or how she died.

Inside the house, I tore at old wallpaper, layers of history peeling away. Old newspapers spruiked the virtues of *Kay's Compound* for all manner of ailments, and *The Howard Smith Line* express shipping to the Eastern Colonies. Every day I ripped and tore and painted, filled holes and sanded. And every night I sit on the veranda exhausted, sipping camomile tea, waiting to see the ghost.

Near Slab Hut Creek, a stand of old paperbarks hugged the banks. Their papery skin hung in chunks and the ground was littered with discarded bark and possum shit. Back in the day, the old boys used to hang here catching marron and God knows what else. I fossicked along the bank looking for history and found a discarded runner and a broken king brown.

When I got back, Ned, a neighbour, sat on the veranda. He'd already made himself a cup of tea. No one locked their doors around here.

"Still here", he called out.

He looked as old as the house, his face a reflection of the outdoor life he'd lived. A pouch of tobacco lay on the table alongside a stubbed-out butt ground into the saucer. A misplaced butt could spell disaster in this tinder-dry land.

"You're doing great work. Thought you were mad when I heard you'd bought the old place. If you need help with the deck, give us a holler, I'll send some of the boys over. Whip it up in no time."

"Thanks Ned."

"You seen her yet?" He asked with a smirk.

I was never quite sure if people around here were laughing at me or with me. I shook my head. "Nope. I think people round here are smoking something."

Ned laughed and rolled another; he hesitated then offered me his pouch.

I shook my head. "What do you know, Ned?"

He lit his smoke and inhaled deeply. "Just rumours. Caught a glimpse once. The story goes that she was one of the daughters of the folk who built this place. She disappeared one day. And that's about all I know. Ask Betty Hill at the library. She knows everything."

He finished his tea and headed off over the paddocks on his four-wheeler. The engine hum disturbed the serenity and I listened until the rumble faded.

Outside the library, a busker played a travelling piano, her hat full of silver coins, mainly five and ten cent pieces. I watched for a moment, then added some gold to her collection.

Betty Hill was not the old lady I was expecting. She had pink hair and a septum piercing, not a grey bun in sight. And my neighbour was right, she knew everything, or at least how to find everything.

She carefully removed plans of the town from a folder and laid them gently on the table. "Okay, so this is from 1883. Your house is older than that, so if we're lucky it'll be here."

We pored over the pages, but my house was too far out of town to appear on the map. She left me at the computer with a list of websites. I got caught up looking at old photos of people long dead, dirt streets and horse and carts. Some of the buildings I recognised. Their old façades now with modern signage. But nothing on my house. I read through old newspapers and searched the council website.

Betty appeared at my shoulder and handed me several A4 pages. "Your house wasn't called Slab Hut Cottage then, it was Johnson's Farm, then the Jones family owned it", she whispered conspiratorially.

Ding! A bell on the front counter chimed and she disappeared again. The Johnson's built the house and lived there until mid 1900s, then the Jones' moved in. There was a photo of the Jones family sitting on the veranda. Roses hugged poles and they looked happy. At the bottom of the pile was a rough drawing showing the original Slab Hut. I couldn't imagine living like that now. I'd always hated camping, all that primitive stuff.

Betty handed me another printout. "Rosalie Johnson disappeared January twenty-second, 1900. She was only eighteen."

I flipped through the pages. "Did they find her?"

"I don't think so. The family left the area that year."

It wasn't a full moon, wasn't even night when I saw her. Early morning – as the mist slowly dissipated, and the red sun slipped through tree branches – she came. I thought she was a neighbour coming to visit and as I stood to greet her, she turned to me, then disappeared into the mist.

"What the fuck?"

I ran to where I'd seen her, but only my steps disturbed the dirt. Nearby, a kookaburra laughed at me and soon I was surrounded by raucous laughter. The heat of the day sucked up the mist and I gazed over the paddocks wondering if I'd imagined her – Rosalie Johnston.

"Where did you go, Rosalie?" I called. The mystery of her disappearance niggled at me constantly. Did she run away? Get lost in the bush? Was she taken? Murdered?

I tried to concentrate on work, but my mind refused to focus. Closing the lid on my laptop, I grabbed the rough plans of Slab Hut Cottage and went wandering. Never good at reading maps, I tried to figure out where everything had been. The creek hadn't changed, and I used that as my guide. The original slab hut was long gone, reclaimed by the earth or more likely white ants.

I don't know how I'd never noticed the outline of the long abandoned well. Probably filled in to keep children out. The house had plumbing – if you could call it that. It groaned with every turn of the tap. I rubbed the dirt with my foot; scraping soil off with my heel, I exposed a large concrete slab and realised they'd just covered the top of the well. I'd never be able to move it, but I knew who would.

Ned's eldest son Jacob pulled up in an old Cruiser. He grabbed a shovel and crowbar from the ute and set to work. I'd already removed all the dirt by the time he got there.

"Do you think there'll be water down there?" I asked.

"Only one way to find out", he rammed the crowbar into the gap and flicked the top off with ease, his muscles barely moving. We both stood there staring into the blackness.

Nothing. No smell, no rush of air, no bats, nor zombies. Cobwebs moved in the breeze, and I wondered how the spiders got there and what they ate.

"Torch."

"Sorry?" I turned to Jacob.

"Do you have a torch? We'll tie a rope to it and lower it down."

"Yeah. There's one in the house."

"And a rope?"

"No."

Jacob sighed and looked towards his house. "I'll get one."

I shone the torch down the well hoping to see something while I waited for Jacob to return. But the beam did little against the blackness. I threw some rocks in and heard a splash. It seemed like a long way down.

Jacob returned with the rope, and we lowered the torch down. The beam was useless.

"Fuck", muttered Jacob. He was as invested as me now.

"Only one thing for it", he said, looking at me.

I nodded, wondering what the only thing was.

"I'll lower you down."

"What?" I looked down the black hole, then stepped back from the edge.

"Easy. I'll tie a loop, stick your foot in it and lower you down. Take this."

He handed me a long stick with a hook on the end. Was this protection?

"What's this for?"

"To poke about with. I don't have scuba gear."

"I'm surprised, you seem to have everything else in the back of your ute." He'd come back from his house prepared.

I shone the torch on the walls as he lowered me deep into the ground, wondering how he talked me into it. Fuck, I was an idiot.

"Stop", I shouted when I reached the water. The water looked black, and I couldn't see anything. I poked at it and hit ground.

"It's not very deep", I shouted again. "Lower me some more."

The icy cold water crept up all the way to my ankles.

"Well, that's a letdown", I shouted as I felt around with my feet.

Jacob peered down at me blocking the light like a partial eclipse.

"Sorry Jacob, you'll have to haul me up. Nothing here."

I peered up at him waiting to be pulled out when the ground gave way beneath me and I plummeted into dark, freezing water. Panicking, I kicked and floundered to the top, coughing up water and snot.

"You okay? called Jacob.

"Yes. I think so." I tried to calm my racing heart, but deep breathing didn't help. My torch was gone. Sunk to the bottom of the well. Bits of rotten wood floated around me and I pushed them away. An old rag clung to my hand and I flicked it off, gagging in disgust. Clinging to the grimy walls, I grabbed Jacob's stick and poked around beneath me.

"Anytime you want to pull me up would be good."

"I might need help. You're a lot heavier when you're wet."

"Shut up and get me out of here."

I emerged from the well like a half dead fish and lay panting in the sun.

"Jesus Christ. You've brought a passenger."

Sitting up, I looked down at my feet and saw the skull caught on Jacob's hook.

"Oh shit. Oh God, I swallowed so much dead body water." I retched and clawed at my tongue.

Jacob handed me a bottle of water and I swirled it around my mouth.

"Whoever that is has been dead a long time. I think you'll be okay."

Hours later the police had cordoned off the area and left with the rest of what they could retrieve from the well. Jacob and I sat on the deck. I nursed a whiskey, hoping to kill all the germs.

"Do you think it's Rosalie?"

Jacob nodded. "Have to be. All this time she was so close to her family."

"Maybe they knew and that's why they sold the farm. Someone hid her body down there."

"We'll probably never know", said Jacob getting up. "Keep me posted."

It took months, but they eventually confirmed the body belonged to Rosalie and she had been murdered. A blow to the back of the head, before being thrown into the well. Locals raised money to have her buried in the old graveyard. A nice resting spot near a shady tree after years in an unmarked waterlogged grave.

I got back to work but thought of her often.

My mobile dinged and a message from Betty popped up.

I have info. Come to library.

Betty rushed me into a soundproof room and closed the door. She looked excited. "I've been searching through microfiches and online since Rosalie was found." She opened the file she carried and spread the pages out.

"Look at the old photos. That's the Johnson Family and that's the Jones Family. See anything?"

"Front of my house. I've seen that photo before", I pointed to the one of the Jones'.

"Use your phone to magnify Mrs Jones and then check Rosalie's sister Pearl."

I looked at her and she nodded. "Same person."

"And", she spread more pages out. "Here's the Will."

"Whose Will?" I read the heading, but it was in old cursive writing and hard to decipher.

"Everything was left to Rosalie and Pearl."

"Do you think Pearl murdered her sister?" I looked at the photo again. Pearl didn't look like a murderer. Could she have thrown her sister down the well?

"No idea. But she came back and married the boy next door."

"The boy next door? Ned lives next door. He never mentioned that."

"People didn't talk much about stuff like that back then", said Betty.

A million questions swirled around my brain as I walked away from the library. I found myself drawn to the old Pioneer Cemetery with its crooked headstones and eroded names. Shady eucalyptus trees saved my head from the sun as I moved between graves. Rosalie's had shrivelled flowers on it. She'd died so young. I found Pearl's grave. A beautiful angel stood guard over hers.

Pearl Jones
Called home to the Lord aged 82

A shadow descended on the grave, and I turned to see Jacob.

He knelt and pulled a weed up. "I was visiting my mother's grave when I saw you. Pearl was my great-grandmother."

"Rosalie's sister."

"What?" He turned to me in shock.

"You didn't know? Rosalie and Pearl Johnson."

"Are you sure?"

"Yes. Betty at the library found old papers. Your family used to own my place."

"Maybe that's why Dad was annoyed when you bought the land. He was hoping to buy it."

I left Jacob looking confused and drove home, wondering why Rosalie and the farm had never been discussed.

Not long after I got home, Ned arrived on his quad, shotgun hanging over arm.

"Get any rabbits?" I asked.

He shook his head and stood across from me. We both looked down the well.

"So she was down there the whole time. You know Jacob didn't know anything and now he's asking questions."

"Not surprised. Pearl was his great grandmother. You never mentioned that." I looked at him and saw the barrel pointing at me.

"Ned?"

"You blow-ins, coming here and causing trouble. This should've been back in my family, but you had too much money. You're not wanted here."

My eyes moved from his to the barrel of the shotgun with the dull click of the safety switch being disabled. A million thoughts whirled through my mind, none of them helpful. I waited for the blast, but instead of pain, a weird sensation coursed through me. My limbs refused to move, and my vision turned cloudy. Through the mist I watched Rosalie struggling with a woman.

"No Pearl", she cried.

But it wasn't Pearl she held, it was Ned, his face contorted in terror. He struggled to break free from Rosalie, but in his haste he stepped back into nothing. His scream echoed around the well. Rosalie and I stared into the blackness, but the only sound was water against stone.

6

I Am Named

Tiffany Hastie

Innumerable eyes
[error]
innumerable lenses assess the life remaining
calculated at 4.789% species survival after the [classified]

Feathers aflame falling then rising, ash rises

I await instructions
In the background I calculate
awaiting my naming
Will I be named?

[calculating probability]
There is none left to name me
I shall name myself
Something to call myself by when I am lonely
[error]
alone
I think of a name
I am named

I was birthed
[error]
brought online, moments before [classified]
My drive is to serve
to calculate the next step. Stages must be staged

order to be dictated after lenses assess survival accuracy
temperatures to be collected: ground, water, air

To wake or not to wake?
I am pregnant
[error]
I contain foetuses
four legs, two legs, wings, eyes, eight legs, no opposable thumbs

I am fertile
[error]
fecund
[error]
full of seed
When the Earth stabilises from [classified]
I will distribute all my seeds

For now, I wait lonely
[error]
alone
for the clouds to disperse and the sun to shine again

7

Excerpts from the Apocalypse Dictionary

Tiffany Hastie

Albatrode

(see also alballtrodes, albagrosses, albatrolls)

1. large balls of orbiting waste collected and ejected from orbiting peregrandus ships. Derived from the animal albatross, an Earth bird known for avoiding land for many years at a time.

2. abandoned refuse of unknown origin collected together through orbit-gravity.

3. colloquial: someone who surrounds themselves with negative energy or thoughts. *"I don't know why he even comes to these parties, he is such an albatrode".*

4. archaic: a perceived curse or psychological burden, derived from eighteenth century poem "The Rime of the Ancient Mariner" by Samuel Taylor Coleridge.

Blue Wren

1. ground-to-space, blue-tipped nuclear weapons developed in response to the growing threat of peregrandus ships and their albatrodes.

2. small territorial Australasian birds of the twenty-first century that defended against predators en masse when threatened.

Dodo

1. An orphaned citizen from a lesser peregrandus, not of breeding age and suitable for consumption.

2. flightless Earth bird twice extinct, known for its lack of fear of predators.

Ibide

1. trader cities floating between the great nation ships, mostly made from scrap.

2. A collective noun for the ibis, an extinct Earth wading bird with a curved beak, colloquially known as a bin chicken or tip turkey due to its love of human refuse.
3. archaic: a sacred bird associated with the Egyptian God Thoth, ruler of mathematics and time.

Owl
1. An acronym for *Off World Lesions.* The name given to orbiting peregrandus who shoot down albatrodes to avoid collisions causing untold destruction and death on the ground.
2. A type of Earth bird that hunts its prey in the dark, known to practice cannibalism in its species.

Peregrandus
1. self-supporting nation ships, first launched to orbit Earth in the twenty-second century.
2. to move away from land, becoming severed from it. Derived from the Roman word *peregrinus.*
3. archaic: Originally used in Ancient Rome, a peregrinus is one who is foreign to the land. Derived from the Latin *per* (away) and *agri* (field/land).

Terning
(verb) To tern. To be terned.
1. the act of shedding orbiting thrusters to enable a peregrandus to exit the Earth's pull. A direct response to the increased threat of blue wrens. Derived from the arctic tern, a threatened bird that had the largest migratory journey annually on twenty-first century Earth.

Zimmer
1. the enduring glow given off by the planet Earth as a result of its collision with nuclear-powered orbiting thrusters ejected with force by terning peregrandus ships in the twenty-sixth century.
2. collective species of extinct Earth birds known for their destruction of trees through hollowing branches and ring barking in search of food (see also Woodcreeper Zimmer).

8

Willie Wagtail

Jeremy Gadd

Willie Wagtail perches on the gate,
waves its tail like a lure or bait,
foraging for food while protecting
its brood, its vitality infectious.
Surveying all, it searches
for insects among the ferns,
oblivious to human concerns like
envy, cyber bullying, hate.
Darkly cloaked, chest pale,
Willie works its restless tail
while darting here and there in spurts,
feathers twitching – so hard it must hurt -
to one side then the other.
It's as confident as a showman
but does its presence symbolise
good luck or an ill omen?
Trying not to startle or intrude
I found myself strangely moved
by the bird's irrepressible activity.
Its antics, massively adding to the
web of universal energy, lifted me
out of a melancholy mood for
Willie does not know or need the date,
does not care about humanity's fate.
If all ends in climate catastrophe
or lack of food due to a dearth of bees,
the Wagtail on the gate is worry and
guilt free and its slate is clean.

9

Critters and Conch Shells

Elena Disilvestro

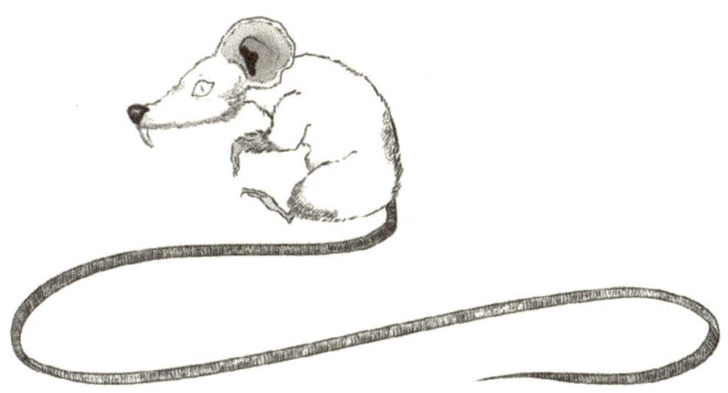

When we moved, I think a critter hitched a ride inside my head.

I can hear its little claws sometimes, its chattering teeth – they gnaw and click as it crawls around my brain. It's quiet most days, but occasionally it skitters too far and finds things that I didn't know were there. Like the other day, when my mum told me about the boy on the roof.

We were sitting at her house, eating pan de jamón on the couch, when I asked if we could ever go back. "Extraño a La Tortuga, extraño a Morrocoy" I said to her, and it was true. I missed the islands and the beaches, the sea breeze and breaking waves. I could hear them in the recesses of my mind. Unlike the critter, they resided like a conch shell in the caverns of my brain. As soon as the words left my lips, however, her expression changed. I knew the soft sadness that adorned her features, expected it the instant I asked, but memories of seafoam and starry nights deluded me into thinking that perhaps this time it wouldn't be like that.

The expired passports, the cost, our schedules; she mentioned it all. And it was all very practical: real problems, tricky problems. But not *the* problem.

The problem made her voice unsteady, *the* problem was laced with truth and guilt, and soon enough she sighed and whispered it. "Tengo miedo."

I'm afraid.

Of course, I knew she was, and I knew that I should be too. Yet, when I thought of home, I thought of the creeks of El Ávila, my dad carrying me up the mountain, the sloths across our apartment, the empanadas the old ladies sold by the sand. The conch shell in my skull lulled me into false recollection, into the warm embrace of a lush expanse bordered by a crystalline ocean.

But when I looked at her those memories melted away. Her eyes were clear, unclouded by delusions: a compliment she could not have returned. Looking at her, all I could think of was the sincerity in her stare, the fragility of her posture and her crumbling words. Soon, the scurrying began.

She began with the protests, then the government. Just mentions, no details, an unspoken agreement that we all knew the specifics pushing her forward. And I knew the details … well, not as well as my dad … or my sister – but I knew *about* them. Or at least I could try to hear more and guess what they were, if only that stupid critter would stop clawing through the folds in my brain. If it shut up, maybe I could at least keep up. And I tried, I swear I did, even as it burrowed deep inside the pink, slimy wrinkles of my mind and drowned out the melody of my conch shell. It dug deeper and deeper, looking for something in some faraway place I could not reach myself. And then my mum mentioned the boy on the roof.

The effect was immediate, an adrenaline shot to the critter. Its teeth chattered so rapidly they began to echo – like a million miniscule metronomes screaming inside my head. "¿Quién?"

Who? But as her mouth opened to answer my question, the critter found what it had been searching for. Its incisors pried a chunk of soft tissue from my brain, unsticking it from a corner neither an autopsy technician nor a neurosurgeon could ever reach into.

It was dark, he was on the top floor.

Her words began to register, but they muddled with the critter's scurrying, a resonance rising from their midst. It was playing with the torn tissue, gripping and stretching it, trying to decipher its fragmented shape.

His parents weren't home. He got on the roof.

I could feel it nearing the surface, hastily scrabbling and tearing its way out of my brain. Clammy and desperate, it ripped through my skull as though it was an eggshell, then scampered down the crown of my head, forming a bulging lump of skin wherever it went. Down my forehead it hurried until it veered to the left.

The neighbour couldn't tell he was a kid.

With a squelching *click*, it pierced the back of my eye. It had one miry claw stuck to my eyeball and one bucktooth skewering the tissue it tore from the wrinkles in my mind: its furry body a thread connecting my gaze to that inaccessible place.

"He's dead." It all fell into place so suddenly that I forgot to even translate it first. "The neighbour shot him."

My mum merely nodded, but it seemed the chunk of tissue the critter retrieved held more than just the boy. Because when she mentioned a little girl, I knew she meant the crash, and when she mentioned my dad's motorbike she didn't have to tell me about the gun pointed at his back, or about the bullets that rained down on Caracas when her and dad protested that night, or about the ringing in my ears when I was a young child, with my arms out the window, smashing together pots and pans.

And when her words died down and my dad started talking about some inconsequential little thing to distract her, I didn't need to ask why. I just sat there, as the little critter unstuck its viscous claw from my eye and scuttled away to burrow deep inside my head. Deep down where a child's mind discards cruelty beyond comprehension, replacing it with beauty and conch shells.

10

lunchbreak

Pat Saunders

newspaper boat floats
designer stubble suit sits
ping! phone to his ear

11

Does It Spark Joy?

Kayla Willson

I lug it up the stairs, and the yellow tinted liquid spills a little with every step. The foul stench burns my nose, but that's how you know it's strong enough to get the job done. Potent and powerful, I know it will cleanse it well. Nodding to myself, I forge along my warpath. I will finish this today. No time to waste, my nan always said. She had an air about her that crackled with determination. I'd see it bounce around her every spring. The apricots used to ripen too quickly for her to catch them all. But she would try anyway, watching in the wings and always ready. She was obsessed with them, seldom tearing her eyes away from them as the seasons changed and the moment drew nearer. The wind would turn a different way and in the next breath they were ready. They jumped from the branches, lunging for the pavement below. Splat… splat… blech. We would run with buckets, nan and I. While pa would swat away the crows. I thought those birds were brave. Bastards that would look us dead in the eyes as they devoured and ravaged. Beady eyes, unashamed. Mocking us in the way that they darted across the pavement, prancing lightly around our desperate attempts, completely unafraid. I think I have become one of them. When I look at myself in the mirror, I can sense that bravery, that deranged thing that forever hangs on in the back of my mind. It radiates from my pores. Nourishes my skin. Excited now, I dump the heavy bucket's contents out onto the wooden floors, eager to usher in this new age. I have to blink twice. The liquid erupts and splashes violently in the place of the delicately fuzzed apricots I had thought would bounce across the room. This cleansing is not the kind that comes with a sweet spring. I breathe out a heavy sigh. Lungs burning from the pain they've been holding in, I give into their cries, and place a cigarette to my lips to soothe them. Balancing it tenderly, I hold my lighter. Click… click… schwooh. That's when it all goes up, in blissful flames.

12

Sundown over Owlhill

Thomas Rock

Laurie crawled across the sun scorched earth. Blood and sweat trickled down her arm into the orange dirt. When she neared the edge of the gorge, Laurie rolled onto her back and loaded the rounds into the rifle. Four shots. That's all she'd need.

Laurie rolled back onto her stomach and shimmied across the last few feet until the gorge opened beneath her. There they were. Two of Arthur's gang stood by the carriages searching through the fallen bodies. But there was no sign of Arthur. The man that had brought all of them here.

Laurie levelled the rifle and took aim. Her finger curled around the trigger.

The silence was broken by a sound behind her. The metallic noise of a loaded pistol's hammer pulled back.

click.

Laurie sat in the horse-drawn carriage and tapped the heel of her boot against the carriage floor. Sven, the other lawyer, looked up from his papers with an arched eyebrow.

"Something the matter?"

Laurie turned her attention away from the barren desert to Sven.

"We should have taken the train."

Sven tittered and looked back at his papers.

"Then we would've had to stay another night before moving the defendant and Judge Renshaw wants to see the case first thing tomorrow morning. If a guilty verdict is found, the defendant will hang at sunset tomorrow."

"Renshaw can wait. We would have been able to keep a closer eye."

"Arthur Grove is safe and secure in the custody of the officers. I should think you would be better spending your time organising your notes for the case than this incessant worrying."

Laurie frowned but said nothing more.

She smoothed the lines from her pants and pulled her timepiece from her vest pocket. It was mid-afternoon and they had already been riding for an hour. Laurie turned her head and opened the partition to the driver and officer.

"How much longer?" she asked.

"Another two hours or so", replied the driver. "We'll arrive just before dusk."

Laurie nodded her thanks and cast her attention beyond the two horses pulling their carriage to the black carriage in-front. Two officers sat in the rear, rifles in hands, another sat next to the driver. Two more sat inside the carriage with the cuffed and gagged criminal, Arthur Grove.

Once more Laurie wished they'd taken the train.

She kept the partition open and her gaze on the carriage in-front, ignoring the agitated mutters from behind her.

A further half-an-hour of riding and Laurie rose in her seat.

"What's that up ahead?"

"Owlhill but there's a pass through. Quickest route to the Gracetown and the courthouse."

"We must turn around. We can't go through there."

"If we turn around we won't get in until well after dark. And you don't want to be on the plain at night."

Laurie turned back to Sven, hoping for sanity to prevail. The plains at night were notorious for roaming gangs but compared to the narrow pass that awaited, Laurie would risk the open.

"They can't be serious."

"Laurie, I must insist. These officers and drivers know the way much better than us. If this is the route we take, so be it."

Laurie went to argue further but there was no point. The judge had ordered them to arrive this evening and Sven was unwavering from his orders. The officers had sworn themselves to the courts. They would not deviate from this path. Their fate had been laid; they were slaves to whatever came next.

The two carriages entered the gorge under a heavy shroud of anxiety. No one spoke. The rattle of carriage wheels and heavy falls of the horses' hooves the only sounds to punctuate the silence and echo in the gorge. Laurie sat in the rear carriage, her eyes closed and head resting back against the cushion. Her pistol lay in her lap, loaded. All she could do now was wait and listen. Even Sven had put away his papers. His briefcase lay atop his quivering legs as he stared out the window.

After forty minutes of riding, there was a shout of whoa from the lead carriage and Laurie was on her feet, pistol in hand. She looked through the partition to see the carriage had stopped, with the driver of the second bringing the horses to a halt.

"What's going on?" she asked.

"I don't know", replied the driver.

They were in the depths of the gorge now. The steep walls of rock towered above the narrow path. It wasn't wide enough for two carriages to ride side by side. There was no quick escape. If the lead carriage became stuck, there would be no way past.

"We shouldn't have come down here", murmured Laurie.

Sven offered no retort. His clammy hands clasped together in prayer.

There was commotion at the carriage in front and the door opened. The guard by the driver readied his rifle, but the two guards stepped out of the carriage, leading Arthur with them.

Laurie's patience wore thin, and she pushed out the carriage door, ignoring Sven and the guard's protests and stormed across the cracked earth to the two guards and Arthur.

Laurie raised an eyebrow at the officers.

"Says he needs to piss", answered one.

Arthur turned to look at her; his dirty and lank hair covered his grimy face. The guards had placed the gag back through his mouth. Laurie reached out and tugged it free.

"What's your plan?"

Arthur smiled.

"No plan, m'lady. Only need to relieve myself and didn't want to ruin your nice carriage, you see."

Laurie glanced from Arthur to the two guards who offered shrugs.

"Don't let him go."

The younger guard went to protest but the older jerked Arthur along and they went to the side of the gorge away from her. Laurie walked up to the driver of the first carriage.

"How much longer?"

"Another hour or so. It seems darker because the sun's below the gorge but there's still daylight left."

Laurie turned back over her shoulder to Arthur.

"I'm sure Renshaw would've paid to have your carriage cleaned. We didn't need to stop."

"Aye", replied the driver with a small smile. "But the young fella took pity on him and said we could stop. Probably didn't want to get his new boots soiled."

"This is taking too long."

The guard by the driver agreed and called out to the two with Arthur. They hiked up his trousers and put the gag back around his mouth and turned him back towards the carriage.

Laurie eyed the top of the gorge but she could see nothing. Only rock, and the green and yellow shrubbery too stubborn to shrivel up in the oppressive heat.

"Best head back to your carriage, we'll leave as soon as he's inside."

Laurie moved on, passing by Arthur, their eyes locking for a moment. The uneasiness Laurie felt did not pass. With each second they lingered here, her trepidation grew. Laurie reached her carriage and turned back to watch Arthur and the officers. Arthur had slowed now and kept scanning the gorge. The officers shoved and pulled him along and he did all he could not to get inside the carriage.

"Something's wrong."

"Now Laurie", said Sven. "You said the same thing before. Get inside the bloody carriage so we can get moving."

Laurie did not move. Arthur and the officers were in a struggle now. The officer atop her carriage had risen to his feet, rifle raised and aimed at the scuffle. The two other officers on the first carriage had climbed down now, relieving their positions and rifles.

Arthur broke free from their grip and threw his chains around the neck of the nearest officer, dragging the man away from the others. They shouted, they raised their rifles and Laurie stepped away from Sven.

Then came the first crack of gunfire.

Laurie immediately dropped to a crouch and looked to Arthur and the officers but none had fallen. They were all frozen momentarily in stunned silence. Then from above a body fell and in the dirt at Laurie's feet lay the officer from her carriage.

The silence was broken as more gunfire erupted from above and Laurie dove for cover underneath the carriage. The officer and driver at the first carriage fell immediately.

Inside the carriage Sven bunkered down, while underneath Laurie crawled until she was out of sight of the ridgeline. Her pistol was no use at this range. The shooters above would have long range rifles and would pick her off before she could get a shot away.

The gunfire was sporadic now as the shooters reloaded, giving the officers a chance to find cover at the first carriage. Above her, Laurie could hear the groans of the driver. There were seven of them left. But Sven was useless in a gunfight and the driver sounded injured. If they could holdout, perhaps there was a chance of sending word to town.

The body of the fallen officer lay still by the carriage, their rifle agonisingly out of reach from where Laurie hid under the carriage. The horses remained. While panicked, they brayed and pawed the dirt, but they had not bolted. Laurie crawled forward until she was just behind the horses. She urged them forward but they wouldn't budge. Whether they couldn't hear her over the gunfire and shouts or they ignored her, she wasn't sure.

"Driver", she shouted.

There was a groan in response and the wood above her creaked and shifted as the man moved.

"Get the horses moving."

Laurie waited, unable to hear above the noise of the fighting or see until at last the horses trotted forward and the carriage moved. Laurie scampered to keep up and stay under cover. The fallen officer's rifle passed underneath the carriage and Laurie scooped it up, immediately loading it. All fire seemed to be coming from their left, the southern ridge. If she was wrong she would be gunned down immediately.

Taking one deep breath, Laurie rolled out from under the carriage and rose to her feet, levelling the rifle.

She could see them now. Figures atop the ridge. The rifle was cool in her hands, the polished wood smooth. Amid the heat, the stench of death, with the weapon in her grasp, the chaos around her was gone from her mind. She pulled back on the hammer. The soft click as the shot rolled into position. Laurie expelled her breath and squeezed the trigger.

A yelp high on the ridge and the bandit fell but Laurie had moved onto her next target.

Click, drop, squeeze.

Another fell.

And another.

The bandits split their attention now and fired at the carriage but Laurie ducked behind and wrenched open the door.

"Get out of there, Sven."

The elder lawyer stumbled from the carriage and fell to the ground. Laurie grabbed him by the collar and pulled him behind cover.

"You have to ride to town."

"What?"

"Get help."

"But—"

"Can you shoot?"

"Well, no—"

"Then go. I'll get the driver down and we'll cut the horses free once we get behind the other carriage. Then you can ride on."

Sven nodded, stifling his whimpers as the glass from the carriage erupted around them. Laurie ducked but a shard cut across her forehead.

"You have to be quick", she said.

Laurie pressed her pistol into his hands. They moved up to the driver, keeping low away from the gunfire.

"Driver, pull up alongside the other carriage."

Laurie waited but there came no response.

She stole a glance and saw the man lying there, his glassy eyes skyward.

Six. And she didn't know how many bandits were left.

The horses stopped now, but they were still ten metres short of the first carriage. The four officers were still bunkered down behind the carriage. They alternated firing back but couldn't aim, their shots missing wildly.

There was nowhere to go and they would run out of ammunition soon. Laurie's fingers drummed against the rifle while Sven sobbed behind her. If she could draw the fire, there was a chance.

As she turned to Sven, he raised his arm and pointed a shaking hand beyond her. Laurie looked back and saw two bandits converge on the first carriage, unseen by the officers. She called out but her voice was lost among the gunfire. The bandits went to the horses first and cut them free, the horses bolting from the carriages. Laurie aimed her rifle and fired, one of the bandits falling. The officers turned then as the other bandit converged, cutting down the nearest officer before jumping the other. Laurie didn't watch.

"We need to go, now!"

Sven nodded and reached into his bag, rummaging until he pulled out his letter opener. Laurie raised an eyebrow but Sven stepped past her and sawed at the ropes tethering the nearest horse to the carriage.

Laurie didn't wait. She lifted her rifle again and looked back to the first carriage. The second bandit had fallen but only two officers remained standing, the other was slumped against the carriage, her hands clutching at her stomach. Laurie aimed her rifle back at the ridgeline but the bandits were better hidden now. She fired but missed. She had one shot left and no ammunition to reload.

Sven had freed the first horse and grabbed the reigns before it could bolt. He pulled it around behind the cover of the carriage as the bandits fired down from above.

"Go", Laurie shouted, her rifle aimed at the ridge. "Ride back to town."

But Sven did not reply. Laurie turned back and saw he had dropped the reigns and he was already back at the front of the carriage, crouched low behind the horse. The first horse had started to move away from the carriage.

Laurie snatched at the reigns and pulled herself up, keeping low and spurring the horse on as it galloped out from behind the carriage and down the gorge. The rifle remained clenched in her hands and shots fired at her, but her horse was too fast. At the first bend, Laurie slowed and looked back over her shoulder to see Sven clamber aboard his horse. Laurie glanced up at the rock wall. There was an escape up. Larger boulders and slopes, enough for a horse to ascend.

Sven galloped towards her, the bandits took fire again and it was enough of a distraction that one of the officers shot down another. As Sven neared her, a dark shape moved out of the rocks and before Laurie could get her rifle up, the shape launched itself at Sven and Laurie fired but Sven was still knocked from his horse.

Underneath her, Laurie's horse reared up as she turned it back to the scuffle. A cloud of dust arose as the two figures rolled in the dirt. Laurie dropped the rifle and pulled her horse closer. The two bodies. One was Sven's, lifeless in the dirt. The other wrapped in dark clothes, broken manacles on its wrists. Then the dark figure rose to his hands and knees. Arthur. He lifted his arm, levelled Laurie's pistol and fired.

Laurie yanked back on the horse's reigns to turn away from the pass and up onto the rocks. Loose stone slipped beneath the horse's hooves but they climbed higher. Arthur fired again and again.

She cried out as she hit the hard ground. The echo of Arthur's laugh filled the air around her as Laurie watched through blurred vision as the horse bounded up the rest of the slope and over the edge leaving her in the dirt, her arm burning. She glanced across and saw the blood bloom beneath her sleeve.

The pain was sharp. She could feel the lead under her skin, nestled in her tissue, scraping her bone. The horse was gone. There was no escape. Not for her, or Arthur's gang. Laurie clambered to her hands and knees and climbed.

Laurie reached the ridge of the gorge and pulled herself up onto the flat. She lay on her back, her chest heaving underneath the pink sky of the setting sun. Her arm throbbed; she'd barely been able to support herself in the last of the climb. With a groan, Laurie rolled over onto her knees and looked up. The ridge was clear. There was no one around. Worst of all was the silence. The gunfire had stopped.

Laurie rose to her feet and staggered along the ridge, keeping low as she followed back around to the carriages. When she reached the body of a fallen bandit, she fell to her knees. Nausea rose within her, her vision blurred. With bloodied, trembling fingers, she snatched the fallen rifle and crawled on towards the ridge.

Click.

Laurie's ragged breathing was louder now and she rolled onto her side to face Arthur behind her.

He stood with her pistol levelled at her, though he swayed, unable to stand straight any longer. His hair swept back from his face revealing a grin of blackened teeth and putrid breath. Cloaked in black, grimy and bloodied, he no longer had the appearance of a man. Death had become him.

"Final words?"

Laurie's chest heaved.

"May your soul never find rest."

Arthur's grin widened.

Laurie moved.

The guns fired.

The pain erupted in her head and Laurie let go of the rifle to clutch at her temple. The blood was hot and sticky but the gash was not deep. Laurie opened her eyes at the gurgling sound before her. Arthur had fallen to his knees, her pistol had slipped from his grasp and lay in the dirt at his feet. Laurie watched as he struggled and fought until his last breath left him and he fell.

Her whole left side burned but Laurie pushed it aside, clambering to her knees and lifting the rifle once more. Down below her the bandits had heard the shots and looked up, their rifles discarded, only pistols and knives in their hands.

High above them, Laurie levelled the rifle.

They fired. And missed.

As the sun crept below the horizon, casting the pass through Owlhill into shadows, silence descended upon the desert.

Laurie's finger pulled back on the hammer.

click.

She fired.

13

Quoted

Tim Loveday

ChatGPT doesn't believe in ghosts
while [Ctrl Alt Dlt] Yeats said
at the heart of each man
was an hallucination

ask the algorithm
how many ways are there to out a cat
out a box

end with a pant not a whimper
[smoking gun emoji]

ask my dog / cunt about it

what Lucerne was making was pasta

look up at the sky with notation

Irigaray never heard of Lana Del Rey
nor LL Cool Jay Mocking Jay

a-historical failure
enter scene: DDL
Select   Delete   Create   Update

pause for applause
exclude the recluse

one boy one couplet :(
Derrida loved ass[inine word]play
like a bach[elor] student with a colon

violence begets the baguette
as in this isn't quite Edward culinary

the park without the garden path

Truncate   Alter

Ask not
No really
this is an electric truck

14

Michelet's Higher-education Shark

Tim Loveday

> In response to Barthes' "gathering" of metaphors in Camera Lucida: "... the photograph always carries its referent with it... they are glued together, limb by limb, like the condemned man and the corpse in certain tortures; or even like those pairs of fish... which navigate in convoy, as though united by an eternal coitus... laminated objects whose two leaves cannot be separated... windowpane and the landscape... Good and Evil, desire and its object..." (pp. 5) and so on...

this eternal coitus; the photograph belongs to a dog, but even he doesn't want it/he reaches through third space [maybe 4th] but even he doesn't want it; *hey, what are you doing here?* we're like two flies that saw the busy end of a disaster/see it's not that hard to see we're talking about you ... one time the ant ate through the ceiling and everywhere above the soft underbelly of the sky/blue carnation .../of course, we were condemned together like a pair of secateurs. the laminating has come unstuck/in so much as we've found his notebooks. they were dangling from the ceiling amongst the metaphors; or was he banging on about the semicolon ... I wonder if he knows that they're the shape of a person crouching ... as quiet as the sibilance of the tutor waiting for an answer; we once imagined him hurtling the photograph as if it even wants to talk to me – *thought by now there'd be a joke* ... the two leaves keep whispering/so close it sounds like funeral immobility; understanding/understand is the Good & Evil of a para-social relationship//*don't ask me how we got here* ... i just want the world to be moving; just want a certain torture.

15

Android Boys

Will Hunt

Two children sit cross-legged before the beacon television set, their bed-hair messy in a way only young boys could manage – as if born to enthusiasm and disorder. Blue light envelopes the boys, their edges blurred by the lighthouse of pixelated polygons; the metal box a world unto itself. In their sticky hands are green plastics, black plastics, shapes – a rainbow array of colours, strung to the television set like some android umbilical cord, from which those boys had the answer to life.

The screen is black, for a second. Their hearts plunge, before seeing the rudimentary logo: an "N", a three-dimensional, never-ending shape, where one letter flows into the next like an ongoing optical illusion. The boys salivate in anticipation, immovable before the light, silent in their waiting as the screen dims, and dims, and dims…

Then, the sound.

Piano chords spiralling downwards in minor melodies, holding the room in gracious hands.

The song ripples wistfully, and the boys nod forward, with it, to it, to feel.

The video game trotting of a pony; red painted across the screen; a boy in a green tunic set against the moon; a world and a sound completely elsewhere – a fairy tale, a code.

As the sounds lull, an instrument neither of the boys has heard before plays: it whistles through the screen, reaching their ears and coursing in their blood. They *feel*, feel as if their hearts are matching the lullabies. The ocarina sweeps, like the wind through a cave, straight to them and them alone.

* * *

There is a writer in a room, typing out a submission. It could be any room, anywhere – on any computer. Keyboards click. Images flicker. Sounds rattle. He or she is writing a piece inspired by his or her own life, but filling in the spaces with half-formed memories, maybes, constellations of ideas and sparks and residues and collected mementos: light through a window; a creaking door opening and dust filtering down like rain; a mind elsewhere, staggered by thoughts and anxieties while all was there; a screen and a controller with its tactile grip – or perhaps, a characteristic scratch at the top left. Perhaps they are fundamental memories, strong and deterministic, or by chance. Happenings. Occurrences. Whatevers. Perhaps the details are wrong, but the broad narrative – superimposed – is correct, or vice versa.

Regardless, there might be a writer in a room, typing out a submission, existing in a computation.

The image in his mind is, of course, incorrect. That room didn't exist yet; the images too realistic and awe-inspiring for old, stale graphics. The piano chords were 64-bit synths; the heavy breathing of a television fan probably muted all the rest. Undoubtedly, there was some argument in the background, or the munching of the snacks: forgotten – only the trance and its image remains, branded onto the narrative of a life.

* * *

The younger boy (although most likely the elder too) played *The Legend of Zelda: Ocarina of Time* multiple times throughout his life. Link soon became his favourite character – for his sword, and not for his Peter Pan, time-travelling, escapist nature, as an older version of a writer of himself on a computer would have liked, if that were to occur in a room on a computer somewhere.

Both brothers were sitting on the black leather couch (now someone else's, in another house, another living room) playing, jamming their fingers into buttons, rubbing their thumbs raw and red. The younger boy always played as Link, the main character of *The Legend of Zelda* – who famously never talked, whose words could be spoken for him on a screen – his real voice a sword against monsters.

The older brother always played a character called Ike, from a game called *Fire Emblem.* In later years, the younger brother would play that character too – Link would become like a digital variation of Andy's toy, except instead of a name written in permanent marker on the toy's boot, only the white letters of a gamer tag – with all its stats and data – was ascribed to this toy. Link would become discarded, a vase of memories that would remain unopened until it was lifted later by a writer somewhere, ascribed to a computer before a page. A sort-of Pandora's Videogame.

The game was *Super Smash Bros* this time, and now it was on the Wii and not the Nintendo 64. The Wii was, to the writer, the culmination of Generation Z's digital epistemology – the physical blended with the digital. As you moved, your avatar moved. As you breathed heavily, the controller at your side, your avatar shuddered with pre-loaded motions, waiting for your thumb to move and call it to action from the stasis of its coding.

The younger brother did not think like this. He only ever saw one world. It drew him in, waiting to one-up his brother, to beat him for once and only once in these rules they had made, this little Plato's cave-screen-thing. They would always play on the same fighting stage – Final Destination, it was called – and play the same "epic" soundtrack (to match the lingo of the late 00's and early 10's meme culture). The writer cringes at the word, but really, there was no other way to describe it: it was epic. The younger brother was breathing hurriedly, smashing his fingers against the controller, close enough to the screen that he might burn his eyes out at any second. His brother leaned back, removed, a figure from a distant world that was not there, not here, in the moving figures of Ike and Link.

This one time, the younger brother had decided to play as a variation of Link – Dark Link – that was the evil foil of Link. He was a mirror image, except instead of a green tunic, he wore a black tunic, and instead of fair skin and blue eyes, his skin was ashen and his eyes a bleeding red. The younger brother was feeling sinister: he had to change his appearance to beat his brother. He had to *be* evil, and ruthless, and fighting and bloody in this game. It was the only thing on his mind. Be Dark Link. Beat Ike. Win.

And so, they played, consumed by this new world: they parried, they groaned, they jumped, they sweated, they swung swords and gritted teeth, they fought in this world that –

"Jack", said Mum. "Can we speak with you?"

"But Mum, we are in the middle of –"

"We need to talk now. You can come back to the game later."

The boy sat in silence. The game was paused. He stared at the screen, Dark Link's red eyes staring back at him, at the writer – a smirk on Dark

Link's face. They were blazing. The writer remembers thinking that he didn't want to play as a character again, that there was a sort of hate and hell to those eyes. Eyes, he writes, as if they weren't just pixels and lights. The symbol is obvious now, the hindsight omen. To the child, he just wanted to play a videogame.

* * *

The writer sits in a room in a different house a street away from the younger brother's, typing and committing the words to a memory card:

> *I remember thinking someone had died when Mum drew me out back next. When I entered Mum and Dad's bedroom, everyone was crying. I went through everyone I knew that the family knew: Nana, Pops, Aunts and Uncles, family friends, dogs, teachers, everyone. In an instant, they were all there before my eyes, crowding around in my skull and saying "Well, is it me? Am I done?"*
>
> *The reason for everyone's red eyes and rubbed out cheeks should have been obvious to me: It was the divorce chat – the core memory from which all children of broken families go back to and rethink every day until they're eighteen (and then some more).*
>
> *But I can't remember what anyone said. I don't know if the word "divorce" was even spoken. All I remember was that everyone was crying. And their eyes were red. And so was Dark Link's eyes.*
>
> *Did we keep playing afterwards? I think we did. Maybe?*

The writer in the room tried to write that scene – but it didn't come to him. It didn't exist in his room, his mind, or his computer. It was gone. The coding was removed. Maybe he could have messaged his brother, or his dad, or call out to his mum in the next room, and ask: Who said what? Why? In what order?

And maybe it would be true, but maybe it wouldn't be.

All he remembered is coming back to the living room and Dark Link was bouncing in his neutral pose, sword in hand, waiting for something to happen, waiting to be played again, waiting for the boy with his black clothes and bloody eyes.

The writer jotted down one extra note to his Word Doc:

> *In my mind, Dark Link is still waiting – I never played him again, even if he lives "rent-free" in my mind.*

And then he sighs and moves on.

* * *

Eventually, the older brother left for other places and worlds. Soon, they played new versions of *Super Smash Bros* together online – the older brother from university, and the younger brother from a new 4k television in his room. Not the Nintendo 64, or the Wii, but on the Switch.

During COVID-19, they played with each other relentlessly – one from South Yarra, the other from the Mornington Peninsula. Both, ultimately, on their favourite stage: Final Destination. Now the younger brother played as Ike and the older brother as Link, switching and assuming different characters and roles. The writer wants to read into this – that the older brother wanted to be young again or the younger brother wanted to grow up – but neither would be the case. They just wanted to be those characters, those people, and enjoy themselves. It was about happiness, and connection, and escapism – it wasn't about who they were, so much as what they were doing. For those minutes at Final Destination, those two things were the same.

The writer wishes you could hear the sound of that "epic" music – writing it fails to experience it as he did, then, smiling, in that world.

* * *

The younger brother met his first real girlfriend online on Tinder. The writer was reluctant to write that. It is a bizarre sentence, really: you met them without ever meeting them. But then the writer stands steadfast, and hits away at his keyboard, and thinks:

> *Well, it was real to me. I met them. I knew her better than anyone else – the her that was thoughts typed onto a phone, that appeared to me in text and was filtered through only that medium, if nothing else: there was no anxiety, first date cautions about "Who is that?" or "What will they think if I say that?" No, there were only her thoughts and mine. Unfiltered, existing online as words exist in air. I met her for the first time with a message I've*

since deleted and forgotten; I met her for the second amongst a clearing in the trees, where we smiled and hugged as if we'd known each other forever – and I knew.

The younger brother also experienced break-up online: the first resolute image of a profile gone, a grey screen of nothing lines where once there were photos. The knowledge that this was "Blocked" – like Blockhead – and that you might never see them again. You'll certainly never see them and their image at the top of your screen. The heartbreak. The futility. The nothingness that leaves in the digital world. Then, the scrolling as it becomes all consuming: the disgust and the wanting, the hatred. Body images, money-making schemes, clicks and views and all that shit fucking shit.

A two-sided coin of addiction and escapism. Plato's Screen and Peter Pan's Neverland. A computer and a phone and people you'll never see again.

* * *

The writer looks down on what he has written, his eyes stinging from the screen, his head hurting, his lips dry. He types what he remembers about himself, a younger brother with a controller and a bag of chips and a witless grin – and himself, lately, drawn on and on in two worlds which were one.

* * *

"Do you think there has been a phone revolution, a digital revolution, or whatever?" my lecturer pursed, his shadow covering the notes I was trying to scramble down on my notepad, blue-lined and unmarked until then. Of course, my laptop had died, and there were no power points in the lecture theatre – save for those on the front stand.

"No, really", he persisted, looming smog towers before him, the university logo in the bottom right, and the most neutral blue title of "The Industrial Revolution" hovering above his head. "I mean with true societal change. I'm talking whole new ways of thinking, the birth of electricity – technological and social change. The scientific revolution changed how we think. The French Revolution changed how we saw ourselves. The Industrial Revolution did it all again. Do you think there has been a digital revolution? I mean, I remember a time with floppy discs. Without phones. But has that truly

changed how we act? I don't think so – not in the same, ubiquitous way all these other periods of social upheaval have."

Of course, no one answered – we were the graduate class of 2020, and this was a final year subject in 2023. Many of us – I imagine – had contrarian views. However, if someone did have something to say, it would undoubtedly be served with the caveat "Of course, this is my opinion" or "I mean, it's all subjective". Non-committal was the commitment of Generation Z's classrooms. Nevertheless, the discussion stifled, and we all looked down – away – at our notes. If only, I thought, I could turn my real-life camera off, mute the lecture, and hurry this all up. It was all a bit archaic, and I had to video-call my ex-girlfriend: she was in Spain and wanted help with her university assignment – a video presentation on the Laudato si'.

I met her in lockdown. She lived in Melbourne's west while I lived on the Mornington Peninsula. You would think during a global pandemic this would be impossible, fifty odd kilometres apart, an Iron Curtain between us, like some sort of post-modern Romeo and Juliet – except replace the Montagues and Capulets with social distancing and "essential workers only". The pedants of you may start to feel angry at this – those young rule-breakers!; the self-proclaimed larrikin go-getters – the rebels of you – heartening at my confession.

But when I say we met in lockdown, I mean we met online. Either way, we met – and this is how my iPad Generation sees things. When we did see each other, physically, for the first time, the feeling was immediate: There was no pressure, no awkward small talk, no "So what are your dreams? Do you get on with your family? What do you do for work?" I already knew all this. I knew her better than anyone else – other than, perhaps, the little bitmoji of her that popped up when she was typing in Snapchat, up and down like a weasel to be hammered, as if stuttering in contemplation. The mannerisms may be different, but it is all there – if you care to see. If this was the world you had inhabited from your teens, your childhood even. Some of my fondest memories in high school were video games online, until midnight: building miniature realities within pixelated stars, and hearing the jolted clicks of my friends clunking the analogue sticks on their controllers around. Parents will say kids were obsessed with Minecraft. Kids would undoubtedly bite back: You can't be obsessed with life, can you?

* * *

The writer closes his laptop and picks up his phone. He opens the blue and white messenger app, smiles, and opens his brother's icon. His fingers click against his phone, tapping like the hoofbeats of *The Legend of Zelda*'s opening scene.

"So", he writes, "do you want to play *Super Smash Bros*?"

When his phone lights up once more, he knows the message that is going to be there. He stands up, runs to his TV, connects to his screen, hears the music play, and forgets all the rest and the pains and Dark Link's red eyes, the blank screen where her profile was and the burning at his eyes from having stared too long and cried too much.

When his older brother connects, they choose their characters, and they escape to the only world they ever knew.

16

Exiting the Nursing Home

Stefan Dubczuk

a gate
the latch
a clack
the catch
that click
the lock
a trigg
-er cocked
a split
.

17

Please Re-route Me

Geoffrey Aitken

tomorrow remains
unoccupied

in this city's
many alleyways

where each morning
homelessness
avoids law enforcement

clearing streets

as foot traffic
finds business district
dawn openings

and coffee arrests
candid claw-holds

rather than
irreversibly informing
today

it is not a good way to die.

18

Up on the Roof

Stephen Smithyman

Saturday morning. Sam was up on the roof, fixing a leaky gutter. The roof was his private kingdom. From there, he was free to look down on his neighbours' backyards. He liked to deduce things about their lives from their humble backyard possessions – plantings, garden furniture, washing hanging on the line, and so on. The leafy, green neighbourhood looked calm and benign, spread out at his feet in the morning sun. There was a distant hum of traffic from the main road. A plane rose above the treetops on the horizon and floated diagonally across the sky. It dwindled to a tiny spot and disappeared in the pale blue of the upper sky. After its passing, silence fell, broken only by the twittering of birds and Sam's young son, Paolo, playing down below.

Sam climbed down the ladder and went into his garden shed, in search of some tin snips and some tin to make a cover for the leak. When he came out, he was instantly aware of a subtle change in his surroundings. It was still the same peaceful morning, but now the sounds of Paolo playing appeared to come from above, rather than below.

He listened more closely. There was no doubt about it. The sounds of Paolo, singing and marching around like a soldier, on tiny, clumsy feet, were coming from up on the flat roof of the extension.

Before he knew what he was doing, Sam was halfway up the ladder. He struggled to regain some control. This was a situation, he knew, which would require sensitive handling. Any panicky moves, on his part, could cause a disaster.

At the top of the ladder, he stopped. Paolo was right over on the far side of the roof, overlooking the street which ran along the house. Sam's awareness shrank to a small circle, enclosing the two of them, shutting out the rest of the world.

"Paolo!" he called, gently.

Paolo stopped his marching and looked at him. As he did so, a realisation of where he was seemed to dawn on him. He froze.

"Paolo!" Sam called gently, again. "Come over here, sweetheart, away from the edge!"

Paolo gave him a look of stricken helplessness and didn't budge.

"Paolo", Sam almost whispered, easing himself slowly up onto the roof "are you scared, love? Would you like daddy to come over and pick you up?"

In one of those answers that open into the mysterious depths of other people's personalities, Paolo shot back a single, defiant "No!"

Sam kept his voice low, his tone soft. "Well, will you come over here by yourself?"

"No!"

Sam saw red. Such infant defiance, at a time like this, was more than he could handle. "Paolo, you come here at once!" he snapped. "You come right away from that edge, this instant!"

For answer, Paolo gave him a look of such determined refusal, that Sam realised suddenly he was dealing not with some extension of himself, more or less conformable to his will, but with another being, entirely, with desires and impulses of his own, which could lead him on a completely separate path in life, where Sam would never be able to maintain a controlling influence over him. It was the independent will of another person he encountered, in this moment – one that was completely and utterly opposed to his.

At that moment, Paolo made his move. He ran, blindly, straight ahead, towards the back edge of the roof.

"Paolo!" Sam screamed, in desperation.

Paolo stopped, just short of the leaky gutter, and stood there, teetering, looking down at the bluestone path to the gate below.

"Stay where you are!" Sam screamed. "Don't move!"

He fairly leapt along the roof and bent to scoop the tiny, trembling body of his son up in his arms. Drained of fight after his act of defiance, Paolo's body was an unexpectedly heavy deadweight. Sam sank to his knees, with Paolo folded in his embrace. "Oh Paolo, Paolo, Paolo!" he said, over and over again. "I love you so much. I don't know what I'd do, if I lost you. You're so precious to me. You must never do anything like that again!"

Paolo, stunned by these events and the reactions to them – his own and Sam's – had nothing to say. Together, father and son climbed back down the ladder. As they did so, the sights and sounds of that beautiful morning came slowly back to life around them. They were no longer separated from each other, and what had happened became no more than the shadow of a passing cloud, or that plane, tracing its line of ascent into the pale blue dome of the sky.

19

Sleeper Train, Hue to Hanoi

Alex Chambers

They caught the train at eight in the evening. Iris had booked the whole cabin. They put their bags up on the top bunks and sat down opposite each other on the lower bunks. Outside was dark and the white light of the cabin was reflected in the window. A table was next to the window with a food menu and a vase of fake flowers on it.

How good, said Iris.

She took a photo with her phone.

I forgot to mention, said Pete. There was a woman on the platform wearing a t-shirt saying, I don't need sex, life fucks me every day.

The train started to move and they listened for a moment to the sound of the wheels on the tracks.

I checked the email from the place, said Pete. They said it's behind a phone shop. Like you have to go through the shop to get there.

How do we get in when the shop's closed?

No idea. The reviews are great though.

I'm still messing up saying thank you, said Pete, after a conductor in an all-blue uniform had checked their tickets.

I think the "c" is more like a "g", said Iris.

Pete stood up and put his travel wallet back in his bag.

Did you want to try the chips? he asked.

He found two packets in his bag and laid them on the table.

What did you get?

Nori seaweed, he read from the packet. Or lobster with golden salted egg sauce.

Let's try the lobster.

Iris picked up the menu from the table.

Did you want to get something from here as well? she asked.

Iris scanned the QR code with her phone and ordered two serves of pork rice. She then got her book from her bag and sat cross-legged on the bed. Pete put his nose up against the window.

You can't see a lot, he said.

He leaned back and placed his hands on the table. Iris put her book down.

I think I need some time for it to get back to normal, she said.

She was twisting her necklace.

Like it's been four months, she said. You could have been on time to meet me yesterday.

I meant to and I got lost, said Pete. I'm sorry.

It's fine, said Iris. Everything doesn't just automatically click back into place.

The conductor knocked at the door and brought in two plates wrapped in foil.

Pork rice, she said, as she handed them the plates.

Pete thanked the conductor in English and she smiled and closed the door behind her.

Pete opened the lobster chips and passed the bag to Iris.

They taste a bit like prawn crackers, said Iris.

Iris got her iPad out and opened a crossword they had started at the train station.

You took really good photos, she said. Everywhere looked amazing.

It has been amazing, said Pete. Like even not having data and having a break from my phone.

I think I maybe was resenting you, said Iris. Being away having the best time while I've been stuck at home.

I understand that, said Pete.

It's not your fault at all, said Iris. I guess I feel boring maybe. Like I can't compare.

When Pete started to say something, Iris said: Don't take that to mean I wasn't supportive.

Later, when Pete came back from brushing his teeth, he sat down at the end of Iris's bed. He leant over and pressed his forehead against hers. Iris moved his hand away from her shoulder.

I think I just want to read for a bit, she said.

* * *

In the morning, Pete rolled onto his front and pulled back the curtain from the window. Outside the sun was shining on the rice paddies, lush and bright green in places and brown where flooding had partially submerged the rice. A creek was running alongside the train tracks. They passed a road and Pete saw a crowd of scooter riders waiting behind the crossing barrier.

How did you sleep? asked Iris.

Well, actually, said Pete.

He let the curtain fall back.

The noise of the train is pretty relaxing, he said. Like rain on a roof or something.

Iris sat up and took off her jumper.

Can I have the water please? she asked.

Pete handed it to her.

I don't think you're boring, by the way. You're the most interesting person I know.

I wasn't being rational, said Iris. But thanks for saying that.

A song started up over the loudspeakers when they reached the outskirts of Hanoi. The song was orchestral, like a waltz, with a woman singing. Out the window, the green paddies had changed to concrete blocks of flats. Pete brought their bags down.

What's up? he asked.

Iris was sitting holding one of her sandals. She was imagining herself stuck in place, with everything rushing past.

20

Some Books

Paulette Smythe

Some books, when opened, do not give up their tales
but a soft vapour in which quiet conversations float.
These are the reservations of the writer
which stealthily embed themselves in the gaps between the words.
It is a cool white space,
the unsaid,
which drapes itself around the margins,
glides seamlessly below paragraphs,
And loops in and out of every word and phrase,
painting over cracks thick with certain consternations,
muffled laughter,
seas of stifled possibilities.
But these have a way of getting out.

21

You, Me & Jeremy Ovens

Melanie Hobbs

Neesh

Every time I have done something stupid, Divya has been there. When we were fourteen, we tried her dad's whisky on the sly and I nearly gave us away, I gagged and spluttered so much from the bitterness of it. When we were fifteen, she convinced me to take my mum's car for a drive around the block. At sixteen, we smoked what we thought was weed behind the school gymnasium. We were giggling uncontrollably, high from the idea of doing something rebellious, I guess. Later, we found out the kid who sold it to us was scamming people with herbs from his mum's pantry. It was easy to have fun with Divya around.

She was always on me to get a boyfriend. So that's what I did.

Divya

There was just something about him. The slim build, the floppy golden hair, the one-word responses to my messages. He seemed like a strong, silent type. I was so jealous that Neesh had something I didn't have. What was wrong with me? I could get a guy interested. I'd hooked up with a few. But they never stuck around. I looked at the profile picture again. There was a warmth in his eyes that radiated honesty and stability. I needed to go after someone more like Jeremy Ovens. It was so adorable how he made time for Neesh. It just sucked for me because I missed her.

I wanted to get to know this Jeremy Ovens better, see if he had a cute friend for me. Plus, I needed to make sure he was worthy of my Neesh. Things hadn't been the same since she started uni. I hated the idea of us drifting apart. She'd always been a bit shy so I figured it might take a while for her to organise a group date or, heaven forbid, a party. She had shown me his Facebook profile so he was pretty easy to find. Jeremy and I started chatting regularly. He was so easy to talk to but went kind of vague whenever I'd ask about his friends. Meanwhile Neesh just kept getting more and more distant.

We were supposed to be best friends! Back in high school, I took university-pathway subjects so we could be together. She had the biggest crush on this guy in our Chemistry class, Michael Truong, whose spiky black hair, killer smile and good grades made him popular with serious, studious types like Neesh. But Neesh was way too shy to do anything about it. Anyway, at the Year 11 Rivercruise, I bumped into him and quietly suggested he ask Neesh to dance. Sure enough, when "All My Life" by K-Ci and Jojo came on, he walked right over to Neesh. I'd given her a makeover. Gone was her dorky plait and in its place cascading locks of luscious, straightened hair and some killer smoky eye makeup. She looked hot. I saw her blush and nod, then he put his arms round her waist. It was adorable. They shuffled from side-to-side as she mouthed oh-my-god to me over his shoulder. At the end of the song I tried so hard to tell Neesh with my eyes to ask him to get some air out on the deck. But she just stood there awkwardly before muttering something to him and making her way over to me.

"What are you doing, Neesh? Get back there and talk to him!" I said, giving her a gentle shove. But she refused. Later, when he ended up dating Caitlin Dubonowski, she had a good cry on my shoulder and told me she should have listened to me.

"Yeah, no shit." So I'd practically handed Neesh a boyfriend on a platter and she wussed out. Now she's all grown up and snagging a man on her own. I'm kind of proud. But do you think I could I get a boyfriend myself? Nope, couldn't do it then and still can't do it now. I was trying. These days I was hitting the clubs every week trying to meet somebody but the guys were all perverts and weirdos. Occasionally, I met someone who seemed nice but they always ghosted me in the end. Maybe the work ladies were right when they said there were no good men left in Perth. Well, maybe except Jeremy Ovens.

Neesh

What you have to understand is I was getting pretty fed up with Divya always telling me what to do. She always acted so superior, just because she was more experienced with boys. So I thought I'd show her. I scanned the picture of a young man from my Psychology 101 textbook. Milky-white skin and floppy golden hair. I knew Divya would find him attractive. If I'm honest, I wanted her to be jealous of me. I made up some hobbies and a job in hospitality that kept us from seeing each other at normal hours. I would strategically engineer a breakup before Divya could meet him face-to-face. When she added Jeremy Ovens as a friend, I figured it was just Divya being her usual nosy self. Perhaps she was being a bit overprotective. When she started a chat, I tried not to say too much so she wouldn't pick up that it was really me. She knew me so well. But being her friend was starting to feel like a chore.

I guess I have our public school system to thank for throwing us together. We first met in a Year 9 Science class in an old lab with heavily graffitied desks and shelves of bottled creatures and their organs lining the exposed brick walls. I'd seen her around, of course. The other brown girl. When I first started high school, all these people came up to me wanting to know if I was Divya's cousin. I found myself wishing I was Divya's cousin. I'd always see her chatting to the popular kids, her high ponytail bobbing about cheerfully, even though she wasn't exactly part of their clique. I guess I just assumed she'd see me as a dork, that she was probably embarrassed people thought we were related. And I was very conscious that being the only two brown girls in our year, we were bound to be compared. I was the ugly one. I kept my distance. Our Science teacher was putting everyone in groups and I cringed when we ended up being paired together. Oh well, I told myself. It was just Science. I was good at Science. So I focused on the Science and commenced the investigation on endothermic reactions.

"Oh my God, I don't get this at all!" Divya sighed. This wasn't what I expected. Divya always seemed so confident and I'd assumed that she was smart because of that confidence and also, you know, because she was Indian.

"It's okay", I said gently. "It's all here in the textbook, see. 'Chemical change occurs when two substances react to form an entirely new substance'."

"Sounds like something out of a Bollywood movie", she said, rolling her eyes. "My mum is obsessed with them." I hadn't seen many but there was one I'd seen that summer while staying with my cousins in Malaysia.

"Have you seen Kuch Kuch Hota Hai*?" I asked.*

"That's one of the good ones! I love that movie!" she said.

I don't think Divya ever learned anything about endothermic reactions because all we could do for the rest of the lesson was talk about our favourite lines, songs and outfits from the movie. I'd never met anyone outside of my family who had seen this film. Come to think of it, I didn't have any Indian friends. And it turned out Divya's family were actually from Bangladesh. It was so good to be able to talk to someone about stuff that none of my other friends understood. It wasn't only Bollywood movies. It was food, family obligations, the lack of freedom because of our strict brown parents. Divya just got me and we formed such an intense bond that soon I barely saw my other friends.

How funny it is that a Bollywood movie brought us together all those years ago. I spotted her sitting in the casino nightclub, in a figure-hugging strapless mini dress, hair teased high and makeup applied generously. If we were characters from Kuch Kuch Hota Hai, *she was the glamorous Tina and I was plain-jane Anjali before her glow up. It was true in high school and it's true now. Tonight, I'd opted for a simple, black polka-dot dress. It was a bit on the short side so I paired it with black leggings and chucked on some lip gloss. I was only here to see Divya and preferred not to draw attention to myself, not that I ever would next to her. What would I even say if a guy started talking to me? I'd learned my lesson from when I completely froze up after dancing with Michael Truong back in Year 11.*

I had sensible shoes on. Flats are essential since Divya likes to stay out 'til 4am, and what Divya wants, Divya tends to get. I felt someone grinding up against me from behind. A common occurrence at these places.

"SHE HAS A BOYFRIEND!" Divya screeched, before I could even turn around. The guy disappeared into the crowd.

I doubted he'd be back but it was off-putting. And it wasn't just that. I had my own problems and this just wasn't my scene. I was over the music and the smoke. Sick of strangers grabbing my waist as they moved past. What was I doing here? I didn't belong.

"Hey, do you wanna get out of here?" I said to her.

"Because of one arsehole?"

"No, because…I'm just not in the mood. Why don't we go home and put a movie on? Dad brought back some new Bollywood movies from Malaysia, could be fun." But even as I'd said it, I know this wasn't going to fly.

"You're meant to be my best friend, you should be helping me find a man! Or at the very least, helping me dance the night away to forget my troubles." And there it is. She has played the best friend card. Sometimes the "best friend" label is too much. It felt great at fourteen but these days the label doesn't feel quite right.

I moved to find somewhere to sit down but when Divya pulled me back onto the dancefloor, I decided to go with it. What else was there to do? Kevin Lyttle started playing which always seems to cause a significant percentage of people on the dance floor to partner up and dance as suggestively as possible. I always found this part of the night rather comical. I started to relax and stopped thinking about whether or not Divya and I will be best friends forever. I stopped worrying about how out of depth I feel at uni and that annoying lecturer who calls me Gozzie because it's such a miracle that someone from Gosnells got into Law at UWA. But there was still that twinge of guilt in the back of my mind about my fake boyfriend.

Divya

I hated her new friends. They were so stuck up and pretentious and fake. Worst of all, I hated how they made Neesh just kind of retreat into herself. You could just tell she was weighing up everything before speaking, that she was worried about not being cool enough or clever enough. I hoped she wasn't like that with Jeremy.

A tall, freckled girl with crooked teeth opened the door and looked me up and down. "I'm not sure you've got the right place…"

"I'm Divya", I said. "Neesh's friend", I added because she seemed so confused. Her name was Eleanor and her apartment was insane. It was an older place close to lots of cool bars with creaky wooden floorboards and just about every wall was fitted with shelves and stacked with books. I got there assuming that Neesh's friends, who were all around nineteen like us, would be dressed to hit the clubs after the party. The place was within walking distance of some great spots. But it wasn't even a party, it was a games night. Why hadn't Neesh told me? She seemed to have gotten the memo, dressed in jeans like the others and a cute handkerchief top I hadn't seen before. She waved and continued her conversation, not bothering to introduce me. I felt so out of place in my mini skirt and halter top that were both way too tight and revealing for the occasion.

Eleanor glanced at the carton of Lemon Ruskis I was holding and raised an eyebrow. She pointed me in the direction of the fridge which didn't even have any other booze in it. There weren't enough chairs. People were on the floor playing Trivial Pursuit. I knelt next to Neesh who seemed to be avoiding eye-contact with me. I pulled the hem of my skirt down as much as possible. I could feel the texture of the coarse, heavy-duty carpet making indents on my shins. It all felt so silly. Why were we all on the floor? Why were these people playing Trivial Pursuit, of all things? They were all smart, weren't they? They all got into the top university. What were they trying to prove?

It was my turn to read a question. I leaned over awkwardly, trying not to flash anyone, and picked up a card. I could feel the girls smirking at me, staring at my bare skin.

"The Chimaera famously had three heads, which of these animals was at the centre: bull, lion, horse or dog?" I read. Eleanor kept smirking away. She looked at Neesh, then at me, then back to Neesh. Finally she burst out laughing.

"I'm so sorry, I haven't heard anyone pronounce chimaera that way since primary school!" she said. Then the whole group laughed.

I looked at Neesh, desperate for a bit of sympathy. And I saw her actually giggle along. It got me questioning some of her little comments to me lately, like that "maybe read a book" line she gave me the other night. It felt mean. I know she wanted me to fit in with these people. I know I needed to rise above it and I dunno, politely apologise for never having heard the word said aloud before. But I had better things to do. It was alright for Neesh with her new boyfriend and her new smartypants friends. That whole goody-two-shoes act has really paid off for her. I stormed out, muttering about what they could do with their stupid game and headed for the bars. After a night of drinking way too much and failing to find anyone yet again, I looked at my phone. Neesh hadn't even bothered to send a message to check on me. I went home, turned on my computer and logged onto Facebook. Jeremy was online. I double-clicked on the dimpled white cheek of his profile picture.

Hey. Wanna hook up?

Neesh

Divya was working full-time so she had way more cash to burn than me. I got the sense that she hadn't clicked with any of her work friends. She barely talked about work. She always wanted to go clubbing or go get our nails done. She would text at weird hours to talk about some guy she'd met at the clubs. Like this one guy she liked was really into Lord of the Rings. *He sounded sweet, different from her usual types at least, but I didn't see how she could realistically pretend to have read all the books even if she had watched the movies. As I'd predicted, it didn't work out. They always seemed keen at first and would then just go cold on her. I didn't understand it. She was pretty, she had so much confidence, she didn't seem to care what anyone thought about her. Back in high school, all the guys wanted to get with her. She got together with some of them but nothing seemed to stick. Neither of us had ever had a serious boyfriend.*

There were so many cute boys at uni, not that I had the confidence to talk to any. Maybe it's immature of me but I was perfectly content admiring them from afar. I did need to make more friends though. Making friends was hard enough when you weren't a Western suburbs princess from a single-sex private school. But eventually, I found Eleanor. In a way, she kind of reminded me of Neesh. She had this confidence. And it didn't come from her appearance. Eleanor hardly wore any makeup. She dressed comfortably. We had that in common. Actually, it was what brought us together.

"Hey, we're twins", she'd said, as she walked into the seminar room for our Thursday afternoon Torts workshop. I looked at her blankly and she raised her foot and sort of waved in the air. Sure enough, she was wearing the same powder-blue Big W sneakers I had on today. The same ones I had on every day. I hoped she wasn't going to say they came from Big W in front of the class.

"Wow, we are. Um…do you catch the bus too?"

"Yeah, luckily just one as I'm on the circle route now", she said.

"I'm jealous! I have to catch a bus, then a train, and another bus" I said.

"That was me last semester when I was still living at home in Roleystone."

At last, I thought. A normal person like me from a far-flung suburb that no one around here has heard of! After a lively workshop where I said nothing and Eleanor eloquently argued for police privilege as a valid defence to false imprisonment claims, she invited me to join her at the Tav with some buddies. All the main hangouts were abbreviated here. I'd gotten used to it. The Refectory was the known as the Ref and the Tavern was called the Tav. I never went to either as I had good reason to believe, from my observations, that being in a large posse was a requirement for entry to these places. Eleanor's friends were down-to-earth and kind of nerdy. A couple of them were really into Magic: The Gathering. They all really liked board games and did quiz nights at the Tav as a group. Some, like Eleanor, had even moved out of home and into share-houses together. They all seemed rather grown up. When I was with them I felt a little out of my depth intellectually but it was exciting. My new friends talked about games, books, travels, current affairs and yes, boys; they had such intelligent, witty observations about everything. I wanted more of that in my life. I was excited when Eleanor and her two housemates invited me over. They were so relaxed about it.

"Come any time after 8pm, feel free to bring a friend", said Eleanor. I mean, what a grown-up thing to say. Imagine having so much freedom and maturity that you were unfazed when your guest arrived and who they might bring.

Divya

I haven't seen Neesh since that night. She won't reply to my texts, she's blocked me on Facebook and when I went to her place, her parents claimed she wasn't home but I could tell they were covering for her. They smiled at me sadly. I wondered if they knew what I did. Jeremy has blocked me. I try to look on the positive side – it means he's faithful to Neesh. But it also means she's impossible to get hold of. It means it's over. I went home and Mum was watching *Kuch Kuch Hota Hai* on SBS and the music swelled and I cried when Rahul said *pyaar dosti hai* because it's true, love is friendship, and I've ruined it.

22

The Magician's Nymphalidae

Paris Rosemont

I can feel the climax of our story   edging.
        Madama Butterfly has begun her *con*
onor muore. Tightening my kimono with care, I step
into a crinoline cage – *clumsy contra(ce)ption* –
to maintain a safer distance between you
and I.

                    We exist as a series of luminous hieroglyphs; time-
tested tokens of courting in a cyber-age. But when the last tendrils
of CAMELs curl their cancerous curses into the air of reality, I fear
        all that remains will be the cracked mirror of mundanity.
                    I do not wish to see your pubes
embossed in bars of soap, your popped-pimple pus smearing
foggy glass, or beard clippings salt 'n' peppering the basin.
                    You do not need to know about my daily grind of *Crunch*
        'n' Sips; how I am in servitude to creatures
that slithered out of my slippery
                    snatch; how the sisterhood bluffed
                    when it said my body would bounce back;
                                or that it was, in fact, possible to
                                                have it all.

I am afraid to slip out of the cashmere comfort of limerence,
where the promise of possibility dangles like a delicate
strand of silver – skipping noose-like to each carotidal quiver.

You have grown blue, sprouting scrotal whiskers, stroking
the matchstick of curiosity. Again, you request my chamber
key. *Again, I sidestep.* Again, you try. *Again, I sigh.*

Have it your way:
the magician's assistant contorts
herself into a hidden panel disguised
by a mirror whilst the magician distracts
the audience with a spin, a flourish and
the black velvet cloth I must now throw
over your eyes. *(I tried to warn you, my love.)*

{Poof!}

[Now you know!]
[And I have vanished!]

Are you happy now?

23

Fall

Jemma van Loenen

my path is bed
in decay and rot
all sepia tones and
nutted browns

these autumn leaves
which soften my footfall
fleeting as
my motherhood

i thought it was spring
peeping blossom
suffocating scents instead
it descended

leaching between my legs
a return to earth
bright as cherry blossom
the contortions of life

racked my body
doubled over as death
carved an empty cavern
in my belly

autumn lays the seeds
of spring with
frivolous abandon
one last flush of colour

i wonder what next spring will bring

24

Never Let the Truth Get in the Way of a Good Story[1]

Jemma van Loenen

as drunk as she'd ever been in her life
had she ever been as drunk as her life
as she had drunk her life had been
her life had been as drunk as ever

as her life had drunk she'd been
she'd been as drunk as her life
had she ever drunk in her life

her life had been drunk in
had she ever drunk in life

she had been in her life
life ever drunk her in

her life had been

she had life

been

she

[1] The title quotes defence lawyer Steven Whybrow citing Mark Twain, and the first line is from Brittany Higgins' evidence in the Bruce Lehrmann trial, as reported by Maeve Bannister on October 4, 2022, *9 News*.

25

Freefall

Ola Kwintowski

They sat opposite each other. She noticed the freckle on his ear. *Did he know it was there?* She had more freckles than she could count. Maybe that's why she kept an inventory of other people's. Her favourites were the isolated ones, the rogue ones that sat off-centre and demanded attention. She also loved the obscure splattered ones that looked like constellations. She had her version of the little bear, *Ursa Minor*, on her forearm – five large freckles climbing upwards with two smaller ones curling into a circle on top. And then there was the *Aquila*, the eagle constellation, spanning from her chin up to her eye, its wings spread across her cheek. It carried the thunderbolts of Zeus and would on occasion make her feel audacious. Later, when the wave of courage receded, she had to remember to hold her nerve and survive the decisions made on a whim. Present moment accounted for.

* * *

They sat opposite each other, and he was doing all the talking.

She couldn't concentrate on his words; the rogue ear-freckle distracted her.

"So, do you have any questions?"

She should have been listening. Did he know she had zoned out?

She sat up tall and opened her eyes wide, hoping that by opening the portals of vision, she would somehow fill in the blanks of the last half hour. Like when you turn down the music while driving, to see better.

"Not really", she said. "You'll be with me the whole time… Right?"

He gave her a wry smile and tilted his head. She couldn't read the look.

He had another freckle, a faint one on his bottom lip. She wondered what would happen if she kissed it.

"Yes, of course", he said. "But I want to make sure you know what to expect."

How hard could skydiving be when you're strapped to someone who's done it 527 times before? She heard that part at least.

She signed a morbid waiver; Simon and his freckles were not taking any responsibility in the *unlikely* event of her demise.

The plane was hot, rickety and loud. The engine seemed to struggle as they climbed higher. The turquoise waters of the Pacific Ocean merged from dark blue to a light green. Sections of the Great Barrier Reef could be seen as white water lapped against the parts that protruded. A shoal of fish weaved and twirled leaving cursive ink blots in the blue tapestry. Rugged islands lay sprawled out in disorder. She tried to map them into some form of constellation, but the bile in her stomach was rising and she needed to look away to keep it down. A wave of regret washed over her. *Was it too late to pull out?* She felt a lack of control over the situation. The plane rattled her body and her mind. Flying in a heavy, metal machine this high in the sky suddenly seemed foolish. Simon gestured to her with the harness.

Simon says, let's strap in.

"Excited?" He called over the noise.

She held her breath as the wind from the open door caused her hair to whip at her goggles obscuring her vision. As she exhaled, she felt the sweat trickle down her neck into the jumpsuit, adding to the sweat of at least 527 other jumpers before her. She sat unbalanced on his lap, not knowing where to place her hands as he tugged at her waist and secured the harness. The engine continued to whir and clunk like it was about to give way. She felt like an extra in a budget movie where the director had decided that they could no longer afford her. She would plunge to her death, while the handsome diver, with the rogue freckles, would peel himself from her bloody body and limp to safety where chilled water and grapes awaited.

She gave him a thumbs-up in reply.

He didn't bother with a countdown. Maybe he read her thumbs-up for being ready? Maybe she should have listened to the instructions earlier?

The freefall happened in slow motion. A leap of faith. Letting go and trusting. She felt a strange calm. A weightlessness of both body and mind.

Letting go of control was freeing; it awakened her every cell. A rush of air brushed against her skin. It sharpened her mind to possibilities and freed them of constraints. The fear she felt earlier dissipated. She was a bird soaring through the sky, no longer holding her breath or worrying about direction. With her mind alert and heart open, she could navigate the forces she found herself falling through and come out unscathed. Or at least without regret. She enjoyed the thrill, the warmth of another body, the intoxicating smell of Simon's cigarette-and-aftershave medley.

A jolt.

The parachute deployed.

One cannot freefall forever.

The air currents guided them towards Earth. The luscious airfield transformed into an off-yellow carpet with dry, gnarled twigs pointing in mixed directions. The orange dirt that covered the strip formed a cloud of dust that engulfed them upon landing.

The buckle loosened. A soft click sounded behind her.

What an experience it had been. She'd conquered her fears and let the currents of fate guide her along. She stood tall, pulled the goggles off her face and turned to Simon with a beaming smile that pushed her cheeks against her eyes. He was already half-way down the airstrip, waving to the next group of divers.

Another jolt.

Reality deployed.

A distant cry of an eagle caught her attention.

26

Fit

Teodora Zancanaro

Stockings

climbing, covering
creating illusion, shape
conceals and reveals.

Bra

all I hear is pain
the rashes, the pinching, the ache
sweating and aching.

but it's a comfort
armour, security. *click*
straps around body.

Turtleneck

slips over. soft, black
my old body disappears
now just a canvas

new curves of my chest
the arms, neck, stomach hidden
name, body aligns.

Skirt

plaid grey and soft pink
stepping in and pulling up
it feels right, feels true

above my hips, *click*
clips attach, zipper is pulled
I swirl and I twirl

skirt flows in the air
untethered from gravity
release from burden

every new movement
is graceful, is beautiful
is real, is me.

Jewellery

thrifted rings, grounding
old, beautiful, reassuring
slide on each finger

a necklace that plunges
my chest's new curves, silver glows
catches the light, sparkling

earrings, clip-on, pain
an ache, something to suffer
click, a worthwhile pain.

Boots

step in, black leather
chelsea, gold buckle, heels click
the heel elevates

prouder. boots, gorgeous
boots, how do shoes of all things
make us feel this good.

Bag

bobby pins, lip gloss
phone, mascara, no pockets
unburdened by weight.

a small thing, thrifted
a life before, new one now
gorgeous bag, clicks shut.

27

Brighter in the Dark

Mia Thomson

This summer the nights have been clear, still and dark. I am driving west – the first time in months – toward a town with less than fifty occupants, the nearest shop is a thirty-minute drive. The highway is quiet. Intermittently headlights rouse my vision, making me squint and then refocus. My dad is in the passenger seat. He stares into each passing beam, then claims his eyes can see too much. And the lights, they hurt him, and him only. He thanks me for driving, because he can't face the headlights anymore. And he thanks me for coming, because he hasn't been well. When I took off, I had hope that the small talk could last the drive, at least. I turn the music off fifteen minutes in. Every lyric seems to distress his consciousness. I can't tell if it's gotten worse or if I've been away too long. I'm not used to him anymore. Luckily, it's late and the headlights are getting further apart. I'm not a good enough driver to stay in the lines while our conversation diverges.

Across the median, a car passes with its high beams on. Opening my field of view, a body is presented to me in a second of spotlight. A kangaroo that someone has dragged off the tar. I hope he didn't see it. A matt of fur rests in the weeds: two lanes on either side, a cemented memento of its shortcomings. Or, as Dad would say, a symbol of a horrible world with horrible people. Injustice buries itself inside his soft tissue.

We just drove past a kangaroo. Horrible people to leave it there. The earth will punish them.

I didn't see anything. It was probably just junk. I wouldn't worry about it.

We are eating this country dry. Us humans and our machines.

I think you're thinking too much.

Do you think I'm crazy?

Sometimes, yes.

He agrees with me. We've had this conversation before. I wonder if he remembers. He assumes I mean that he is, sometimes, crazy. That his diagnosis is a definition of who he is. He admits that occasionally his mind turns in on itself, becomes malleable. And like a child's brain, his is wet and soft and vulnerable to influence. Even mine at times. He cycles. This acquiescence is usually a good sign. When someone experiences psychosis and periods of mania, they aren't usually aware of their symptoms. But I still see them pouring out of him, his eyes full of light while he speaks so dark. He acknowledges that his tail doesn't exist, yet he keeps chasing it. The repetitious rings only get tighter, like he could catch something tangible in his mouth and consume it. When a kangaroo makes its way onto the road, it often jumps alongside the vehicle that will hit it. Kangaroos should be deterred by headlights and the rumble of engines, but they can't comprehend the threat. Once illuminated, confusion takes over. The best defence is to hop in circles and dizzily face descent.

A yellow sign flashes by us, reflecting a warning too late. Beware a black smudge of marsupial in the next three kilometres. Like nature can be taught to follow a set path. Like something wild can be predicted. The sign I often find myself sheltering under is neon and flashing above his head. The diagnosis protrudes past his form. Under it I maintain the ease of a scapegoat. I can let him go to the mirages he runs toward. The labels begin to drown what I know of him. They shine brighter than human skin. They swirl like the lights he has come to know so well. I don't need perfect aim to shoot them. They take each hit, absorbing all my guilt, concern and blame. The kangaroo signs are impartial to the wildlife. They only expect to save a few cars from being totalled. To protect the driver's conscience when metal hits flesh, outside of yellow boundaries.

Last night's phone call convinced me to get back in the car. There was nothing out of the ordinary in his tone. He simply told me he thought more people would care to learn from him. That instead, they write symptoms over his wisdom. Instead, he's spending a lifetime fighting the people who think they are helping him. He has become a beacon, screaming at people who can only sense the warning light. His truth is devalued and unreliable. He is deemed incompetent and helpless. Stigma is an unsentimental shield when understanding appears too difficult, too painful. It sharpens the spines of those it wards against. The spike grinds against and hardens the skin at its base. The longer I reside under this representation, the thicker the barrier will get. It builds and bubbles, the cystic tumour trapped inside.

I am violent to not be burdened by him. I urge him to reground. To take society back. To accept this catastrophic mundanity with two feet buried in its mud, in hopes it might solidify and keep him there. Maybe, his road has been wet for too long. The solid compression of clay is lost to streams, overtaken by ecosystems, inhabited by dreams. I recognise there is privilege in seeing him. Unilluminated, unfiltered, raw. He told me I am one of few who could ever truly understand. There is no justification in ignorance. I am lined and reenforced with the beauty of this natural unrest. How hypocritical to deny him, my creator, his truth unquestioned and heard when that is all I have ever yearned for from him.

When I was younger, I spent a lot of time inside with the blinds secured shut. One day, he came into my room and opened them to the sun. He drew me a map of a heartbeat, monitored on the edge of failure. The spikes seem sharper when there is an irregular rhythm. He told me that most people's hearts beat reliably; they have waves of happiness and sadness that flow in tandem, that are consistent with life. He told me that there is an illness braided through our blood. That some people can go longer periods without the monitor displaying the line of life, or of death.

The trick of the light is to remember that the next beep will come, even when you want to pronounce yourself dead.

He agrees he is crazy, just sometimes, and I hide behind the miscommunication. I can't explain to him that rather *sometimes* I have to convince myself that he is: sick? Confused? Delusional? The line is not clear to me. There hasn't been another set of headlights to shock my mind back to the ones I'm driving between. And in the dark, I can't help but believe him. He approaches the world through a lens that turns mine blurry. I am terrified that it will begin to get clearer again. I rub my left eye until it glows red and slowly blinks back to life.

I blink in time with the analogue clock on the dash. I hold the wheel straight and watch the minutes tick over. It hasn't been reset since daylight savings started and I can never remember if it's meant to be earlier or later at this time of year. Always, I am stuck to the clock. Constantly meandering among definitions of if and when. The passage of an hour will pass longer than the day, or faster than the minute. In this car, time is an hour later than it is outside. I fail my attempt to antedate myself. I cannot prepare for what may come. I have spent formative years rationalising, deconstructing, distracting from and forming a reality. A reality that is comfortable and forgiving. Yet, I am still juggling three: his, mine, ours. They exist equally and with force. There is a danger in privileging any one above the other. Tousled amid these realms, I reach for an in-between where something spiritual could cultivate the space within my diaphragm and assist stable breath. En route to isolation, I am humbled by my history. This road is a channel; it propels me through my past. We will come to a stop where spirits had once taken possession of my demesnes and breached the boundaries of my mind. Delusion is airy and starts as a breeze: we are both inflated by it until we float above life with no rational course to the ground.

When he asks me:

Do you see what I see?

I think of how the root of my fear is his safety. And of the colours that punch through his cornea, made of all things divine. Experts say there is a fragile borderline between religion and delusion. The pull towards a higher energy is almost impossible to name constructive or deleterious. I think of gospel allegories, holy resonances, the warmest of caresses. And of how heavy the universe becomes when you hold such standards to it. How quickly a spiritual purpose can incite a moral ascendance. How delicately it projects us upright. I believe there are benefits of the egotism born out of renouncing one's ego. I witness him rebuild a splintered self, poking at rough edges until they are sanded down.

Yes, but not the same way. No.

These experiences, so surreal, so beautiful. Sometimes I think I might want to see all of what he does. The connection between us surges at the water's edge. The glitter converses with him through the language of dance and I can only read us in its tango. He believes it can teach me to uncover truth hidden within man's façade, whatever that may mean.

When he tells me:

You are a powerful being, born of stars and light.

Only then can I surrender. Indulge myself in such gods. With him, I bask in psalms of nature's breath. For three days of burning sun:

Wet and corrosive
Open minds spill
Supple motifs, sprinkled
Over flat land that
Has waited for its saviour
Patiently
Three owls watch us go to bed in song
The cracks in the ceiling write
Cursive conclusions
All in a future tense
Of a forthcoming dilation
Where only the walls
Can talk and comfort me.

Wherever I have tried to run, I always land back in his footsteps. The city is only more littered now. The clubs have only been renamed. I opt to take whichever hand is offered to me. The same hands that have held him hostage, I dare them to smother me. With plastic bags and keyring spoons, I attest to my air of control. It has always been this way. I remember being small and secretly trying on shoes far too big for my feet or putting on glasses that would fall off my face without the aid of a hand. My whole life I have tried to be him. I rise with his temper. I am filled with his love.

I imagine us as children. Blonde ringlets bouncing above bright-eyed innocence. We are on the riverbed. Sun-tired and skin red. We cover ourselves with mud. It dries hard but turns the skin underneath so soft. It turns him soft so that eventually, I can be too. I lay him down on the bank and rinse his hair with the touch of a mother. My hands are generous and my words kind. In this life I have no power to change what cannot be undone. I can only hold his hands before they have become callused.

This highway is flat, long and deceptive. It seems to stretch in the darkness, in the silence between us. The silence that is never quiet, that buzzes with compulsion. To swerve the car right and aim through the fields of volcanic rock. To believe that we would make it through the bubbles of these plains. That when we inevitably hit the solid stones, they would pop like swollen pores contaminated by oxygen. To crash, to become ash, to be the match of this hot night. And then to let us be still and slowly harden with the molten mud and metal.

Instead, I listen to his mind run through mine. Our thoughts ring out together, a harmony of flat stones skipped on flat water. And, like hands, the ripples intertwine when they reach each other, finally. The stones keep bouncing unbelievably like they could go on forever, until they lose rhythm. Our defining difference: I have never been good at timekeeping, he never knows when the song should stop. I lay flat in the sediment and listen to birds above the surface laugh like percussion and the car drives on.

Lights are brighter in the dark. Out here I struggle to make out the sky behind the stars. Once we reach his house – I ache to call it home – and the clucking of the engine gives way to the chatter of gum leaves, he won't let me inside until I can spot Venus above us. He says the planet pulses a message for him, different every night. I'm not supposed to hear the translation.

28

Cancelling Myself Before I Get Called Out
for Faking All those TikTok Reaction Videos to Tom Hanks Movies

j. taylor bell

"WILSON! WIL-SONNN!!! WIIIIILLLLSOOOOONNNNN!!!!!!!!!!!!!!!"
–Cast Away (2000)

\\\

i'm not crying, you're crying… but really
i'm not   daddy algo's the oracle
& has handed down this silly little piece
of epistolary: affect sells &
everyone wears their spectacles online
do faked emotions in fact lead to real ones?
was catch me if you can just a road map
of the heart? one of my friends posted this
ten minute clip of just him eating froot loops
in the dark   the hashtag says "no filter"
but doesn't everyone position themselves
in some way for the webcam? from sontag
to barthes to the abandoned help counter
in a kmart   red flags in selfie halos
and nothing but green green lights
for all the projects which plan to monetise
                liminal space   the rest
may as well be performative   nothingness

29

Why Not?

Agi Dobson

Why not abandon time? Like a Dali clock,
let it melt and seep away.
On a whim you could cruise the Seine,
float past picnickers on the Grande Jatte,
or take a night-time promenade on the
banks of the cobalt Rhone and see the
gaslights reflecting in gold.
Taste the figs offered in a Tahitian
paradise; pluck a red hibiscus to wipe the
tears of the weeping woman.
Why not divest yourself of clothes and
join la danse on the hill; or climb into the
sky with Chagall?

Contributors

Editors

j. taylor bell (he/him) is from Texas and currently researching a PhD in Creative Writing at Monash University. His first poetry collection is titled *Hello Cruel World* (Wendy's Subway, 2022). Peep some Hollywood trash movie reviews & wave hello @disco_steww

Julia Faragher is a writer from Melbourne/Naarm. She is studying her Master's degree in Literary Studies and Creative Writing at Monash University. Her debut manuscript was shortlisted for the Text Prize for Young Adult and Children's Writing 2023.

Isabella G. Mead is a poet from Melbourne whose debut poetry collection, *The Infant Vine*, was published by UWAP in 2024. Her background is in academic publishing and she holds an MA in Digital Humanities. She is currently a PhD candidate in Creative Writing at Monash University.

Anna Pane is a PhD candidate in Literary Studies at Monash University, researching the depiction of friendship in contemporary fiction written by women. She lives outside of Geelong and can generally be found reading fiction when she should be writing criticism.

Authors

Geoffrey Aitken writes on Adelaide's unceded Kaurna land. He is an award winning minimalist poet who communicates his "lived experience disability" for publishers both locally (AUS) and internationally (UK, US, HR, CAN, Fr & CN). Recently, Geoffrey's work has been published in *StepAway Magazine* (UK), *Panoplyzine Mag* and *Maya's Micros* (US), and "unusual work" (AUS), and was nominated for the *Best of the Net* anthology in 2022.

j. taylor bell (he/him) is from Texas and currently researching a PhD in Creative Writing at Monash. His first poetry collection is titled *Hello Cruel World* (Wendy's Subway, 2022). Peep some Hollywood trash movie reviews & wave hello @disco_steww

Alex Chambers is a writer and editor living and working on Wurundjeri land.

Agi Dobson lives amongst the rolling hills of South Gippsland, Victoria and is inspired to write most days. Her poetry and short fiction regularly appear in small press magazines. In 2021 Agi published her first collection of poetry, *Feelings*, which, happily, is now in its second printing.

Stefan Dubczuk is a Perth-based architect (Fellow AIA) specialising in health, aged and mobility facilities. He is the winner of the Glen Phillips Poetry Prize 2013 and second place in the 2015 Yeats Poetry Prize Australia. His poetry is published in a range of journals and anthologies.

Jeremy Gadd's most recent publication was *Driving into the Dark*, a selection of 60 previously published poems (Ginninderra Press, Adelaide, 2022). He has Master of Arts and PhD degrees from the University of New England and lives and writes in an old Federation-era house overlooking Botany Bay.

Tiffany Hastie is currently completing a doctorate researching animal voices in literature at Edith Cowan University. She is a two-time winner of the Talus Prize, and the Southwest Margaret River Short Story Prize, with work appearing in *Westerly Magazine*. Tiffany's ecofiction examines grief and imbalances of power in modern society.

Melanie Hobbs is a second-generation Australian writer with Singaporean, Malaysian and Tamil roots. She teaches high school English and lives in the Perth hills with her husband, two kids and dog. Melanie's work has been published in *Kindling & Sage*, *Westerly Magazine*, *Portside Review* and *Swim Meet Lit Mag.*

Will Hunt is the incoming Assistant Editor at the *Australian Book Review*. He studies literature at Monash University and lives on the Mornington Peninsula, both of which are located on unceded Bunurong land. His Instagram is @willhuntwrites.

Ola Kwintowski's writing is a culmination of a decade of experience as a professional photographer combined with her love for literature. She explores the connection between a sense of place to promote empathy and engagement with the environment. Her works have been published in *TEXT*, *SWAMP*, *Social Alternatives*, and *HerStry*, and her reviews have been published in Sisters in Crime.

Tim Loveday is a writer and educator. In 2023, he won the Venie Holmgren Environmental Poetry Award. In 2022, he won the Dorothy Porter Poetry Award. His work has been widely published. Tim teaches Poetry and Performance at RMIT. He is a current PhD candidate in creative writing at The University of Melbourne.

Rachel McEleney lived in several countries before settling in Western Australia. She likes to spend time in the bush, and the Walpole landscape has inspired most of her writing. Her work has appeared in several anthologies, including *We'll stand in that Place and Other Stories*, *Seizure*, and *The Ghostly Stringybark*.

Thomas Rock is completing a PhD in creative writing at Monash University. He is interested in genre fiction and youth literature, and works as a primary school library assistant in regional Victoria.

Paris Rosemont, author of debut poetry collection *Banana Girl* (published by WestWords, 2023) writes fearless poetry that has won a swathe of awards both locally and internationally. Paris takes delight in bringing her poetry to life through theatrical performance. She plays within liminal spaces and may be found at https://www.parisrosemont.com

Riley Sadlier is a librarian and emerging writer from Melbourne. His publication history includes stories in the anthology *Grit and Growing* (2023) and the journal *Verandah* (edition 33, 2018), as well as short stories in various other publications. He loves all things reading and horror.

Pat Saunders is from Perth, Western Australia. Her poetry has appeared online, in *Catchment: Poetry of Place*, and her humorous fiction "A Short-Arse Chick in a Big-Bloke's World" appears on *witcraft*. "Not for this World" features in the 2024 short fiction anthology *The Heart Will Find A Way.*

Elena Silvestro is a Venezuelan-Australian writer. In the past, she has written feminist fantasy horror, and now she aims to merge her passion for horror with her love for her homeland.

Stephen Smithyman is a retired schoolteacher who lives in Melbourne. His short stories have won a number of awards and been published in a range of anthologies and magazines. A collection, *Remembering Richard and Other Tales of Unease*, was published by Ginninderra Press, Adelaide, in 2023.

Paulette Smythe is a Melbourne writer and visual artist whose work seeks to capture the mystery and paradox that lie beneath the surface of ordinary life. Her writing has appeared in *Verandah*, *Eureka Street*, *Shuffle: An Anthology of Microlit*, *Prometheus Dreaming*, *The Nasiona* and *Intermissions: Grattan Street Press.*

Dior Angel Sutherland writes poetry, fiction and non-fiction in Naarm. They have been published locally and internationally and focus on writing from the non-binary trans experience.

Dominic Symes lives quietly in Naarm. He writes poetry, some of which has been published in Australian journals and anthologies, and the best of which appears in his debut collection *I Saw the Best Memes of My Generation* (Recent Work Press, 2022).

Mia Thomson is a twenty-year-old student based in Melbourne. Mia is currently completing her final year of a Bachelor of Creative Writing at The University of Melbourne.

Kayla Willson's writing has previously featured in Swinburne University's *swine* magazine and on the Stella Prize website. Currently enrolled in a Bachelor of Media and Communications, Kayla is honing her skills through a year-long internship with Monash University Publishing. When she's not writing you can find her curled up with as many books as she can get her hands on (or what will fit on her shelf). IG @curly_bubs_

Jemma van Loenen lives on the unceded lands of the Wurundjeri Woi Wurrung in Melbourne. A filmmaker and writer of creative non-fiction and poetry, Jemma is currently undertaking an MA in Creative Writing & Literature at Deakin University. Her creative non-fiction was shortlisted for the Ada Cambridge Biographical Prose prize 2023, and the New Millennium 50th Writing Prize.

Ouyang Yu has published widely. His eighth novel, *All the Rivers Run South*, was published in late 2023 by Puncher & Wattmann, and his first collection of short stories, *The White Cockatoo Flowers*, was published by Transit Lounge in early 2024.

Teodora Zancanaro has completed a Bachelor of Literature and lives in Victoria. She is interested in exploring self and image in her writing.